Cassie Gets it On

Mary Tales Collections, Volume 4

Mary Tales

Published by Mary Tales Books, 2017.

CASSIE GETS IT ON

First edition. August 6, 2017.

Copyright © 2017 Mary Tales.

ISBN: 979-8231233427

Written by Mary Tales.

Cassie On Video

Cassandra, or Cassie, as she preferred, had a beautiful face, heart shaped, with big blue eyes, small, perfect nose and lips made for smiling and kissing, all framed by a bob of dark blonde hair. But the lovely face was, if not upset, certainly disappointed. "I don't know if I want to go to Japan now." she announced.

"He must be good." Maria said, smiling at her cousin.

Cassie smirked, and went a little red. "Next week, I'm going to Japan for four weeks. That'll be longer than I've been with Noel. It's just such shitty timing." She sighed and stirred her tea. "Single for two years, and then I go and meet the perfect man three weeks before work sends me on the trip I've wanted to do since I was fifteen."

"I'm sure he'll wait for you."

"Oh, he will. It's just that I've just got used to having sex again. Four weeks without it, and I think I'll explode."

"Two years single. I'm sure you've got some toys you can take with you."

"It's Japan, I was planning to buy some toys when I got there. They're very inventive."

"You're not the little girl who was my bridesmaid any more, are you?"

"Maria, I was nineteen when I was your bridesmaid. I was already having sex."

Maria put her hand to her mouth and feigned horror. "Say it ain't so. Say it ain't so."

"I can't believe that was five years ago. How was your anniversary?"

It was Maria's turn to flush, though her expression suggested it was with happy, and naughty, memories. "We had a lot of sex. I'm not telling you anything about the sex."

"But, dear cousin, how am I ever going to learn about sex if you won't tell me all about it?" Cassie said.

"Just ask Noel, I'm sure he'll be very happy to show you. Anyway, you're obviously having lots of sex. So much that you only just got round to telling me about it. What is the wonderful Noel like?"

"Well, he's thirty two. Everyone likes to comment on the age difference."

"It's not a huge difference. Not compared to some of the couples I know."

"He used to work with my old flatmate, and she introduced us. I think I owe her an apology for going to her party then spending the whole night talking to him. We don't live very far apart, so we shared a taxi home."

"Oh yes?"

"No, we didn't just jump into bed right then. We went for a few drinks the next day. And jumped into bed after them. He's just lovely. He's very masculine, like tall and strong and practical, but really sensitive too."

"He has that perfection only a new lover can possess."

"Don't be mean. I'm in love."

"When do I get to meet this wonderful man?"

"After I get back from Japan. Any time I have with him before then is going to be spent in bed."

"So why on Earth am I keeping you from him?"

"Because Thursday is when they list most of the stuff they sell and write a bunch of new content for their website, so he'll be busy until nearly midnight. So I wanted to tell my favourite cousin about my new man and then get some shopping done."

"Last minute Japan shopping?"

"I really need a new camera. Noel offered me one of his, but it was an SLR and it was too big and I'd probably spend my whole time there learning how it works. He did suggest some good small cameras I should look at."

"You'll get something really cool if you wait until you're in Japan to buy it."

"I don't think I've learnt enough Japanese to cope with technology shopping in Akihabara." Cassie stared into her mug. "Well, I'm almost finished. Do you want to come camera shopping with me?"

✳ ✳ ✳

CASSIE WAS A DECEPTIVE woman. She had such a slight figure that it wasn't until you stood beside her that you noticed she was taller than average. Maria mused that her cousin still looked like the sweet young girl who had caught the bouquet, then blushed a bright red, five years before. But she carried herself with more assurance now. That might have been because she was getting laid. Or it could have been one of the things that got her laid, it was hard to say.

Cassie had a list of cameras to choose from, and found most of them in the nearest electronics shop. "It's between this one and that one over there." she said after examining them all for a few minutes.

"You could toss a coin." Maria suggested.

"I like the feel of this one, it's a bit heftier. And it shoots high definition video. I reckon I can find a use for that."

"Pricey, though."

"I've been saving up. I'll have one of these. I can't believe we've not been bothered by any salesmen yet."

"Oh, I've been glaring at them to keep them back while you made up your mind."

"Stop glaring, then. I'm ready to buy."

"I expect a picture a day, at least, whilst you're over there." Maria said as they left the shop. "It's time for me to head home. Do you have anything else on your shopping list?"

"No, only this, really." Cassie looked into the bag she was carrying and smiled. "I think I'm going to go home and test this out." She had the expression of someone who had just had an idea, but couldn't decide whether it's brilliant or ridiculous.

They hugged and went their separate ways. Cassie wandered dreamily to the bus stop and rode home running an idea through her head. Clutching the bag with the camera in close to herself, she thought about the ways she could use it. Before she left the country, she had decided, she could put together something for Noel to remember her by.

Back in her flat, Cassie unpacked the new camera and read the quick start instructions. She started charging the battery and went for a shower. The light on the charger was green by the time she returned.

The living room wasn't the right place. Her flatmate was out, Thursday was one of the nights she regularly stayed over at her boyfriend's, so she wasn't going to interrupt, but her laundry was drying on racks by the window and in front of the radiators. The room was too messy. Cassie took the camera to her bedroom.

There was only a single bed in Cassie's room. It gave her more space for a desk and storage, and she hadn't been expecting to need a double. It would be very cosy sharing the bed, but she hadn't had Noel stay over yet. He had a double bed and lived by himself, so his place was always a better option.

After a quick study of the camera's instructions, Cassie worked out how to record video. She placed the camera on her desk, pointing at the bed, and set it recording. Sitting on the edge of the bed, she looked into the lens and wished she had thought more about how she was going to do this.

She should have chosen something better to wear- better to take off- she thought. As it was, she only had on an over sized blue T-shirt and plain white knickers. If she stopped and went looking for alternative clothes, she knew the momentum would be gone and she'd never get the video shot.

"Hi. I got one of the cameras you recommended, and I thought I'd try it out. I thought you might like a little something to remember me by while I'm away. I'm going to miss you so much, and...." Not knowing quite how she wanted to finish the sentence, Cassie stood. She turned around and, over her shoulder, said, "This is what you have to look forward to when I get back from Japan."

Reaching down, Cassie took the hem of the T-shirt and lifted it until her knickers were revealed. She was rotating her hips to a song in her head, a combination of stripper tunes she half remembered from films and TV. A flush of excitement ran through her, from her groin outwards, and she could feel her skin warming and nipples tightening.

The T-shirt was up as high as Cassie's breasts now, and she could feel the long, stiff nipples through the material. She pinched them through the cotton, and rolled them between her fingers. It made her shiver, and a little pulse travelled from her crotch to the sensitive points. Cassie laid her head back and let out a little sigh. Her back was still to the camera, her viewer would have to imagine what she was doing. She pulled the T-shirt off and stretched out her arm slowly to drop it, looking back at the camera as she did.

Rotating in time to her imagined soundtrack, Cassie turned to face the camera, grinning at it because she had her left arm across her chest, shielding it from view. She imagined Noel watching her on the screen, knowing he couldn't touch her when that was what he wanted the most to do. It turned her on.

Cassie sneaked her right hand up to cover her right breast, without revealing it in the move, then put her left hand on her left breast. She squeezed them, then spread her fingers just enough for the nipples to pop between them. Pressing the fingers back together, she caught her nipples and tweaked them. The sharp feeling tugged at her crotch, and she knew she was hot and wet and ready.

But the tease needed to go on some more. Running her hands up to her neck, Cassie revealed her breasts, squeezing them together with her elbows. Then she ran her hands through her hair, piling it on top of her head, then pushing it one side then the other. Arms out wide, she pushed her chest forwards. Her excited nipples stood proud at least half an inch, pointing slightly away from each other and up a little. Her breasts were barely a B cup, small and firm and sensitive, perfectly in proportion with the rest of her body. She liked them just the way they were and, importantly, so did Noel. Clasping her hands behind her head, she let the camera get a good shot of them for him to enjoy.

Cassie's hands came down again, sliding along the slope of her breasts until she could tweak her nipples, then continuing to her belly then the top of her knickers. Gently, she pushed the waistband down her hips, tugging the triangle of material with it. When the first hairs of her neatly trimmed bush came into view she stopped.

The fingers of her right hand sneaked under the waistband of her knickers and Cassie pushed her hips forward as they explored lower and lower. She ran them through her short pubic hair, then rubbed the sheath over her clitoris. This made her shiver, a mini orgasm tingling through her body. She moved lower, down to the warm, puffed up lips of her sex, and then into it.

Cassie's pussy was wet and hot. Her fingers slid in and out easily, warming her and turning her on ever more. She rarely got this turned on without help. Noel's tongue and fingers could do this to her, but not her own hands.

It had to be the camera. Cassie knew that Noel was watching this, some time in the future. She imagined what it was doing to him, turning him on, making his lovely cock hard. So hard he had to reach down and let it loose, play with it, rub it up and down.

Cassie came. A little orgasm making her press her thighs together, clench her buttocks and bend at the knees and waist to keep it in. She let out a whimper of joy.

"See what you do to me?" Cassie said to the camera lens when she was able to look up again. Her breathing had sped up, and her cheeks were warm with a happy blush. "I think I need to sit down for a while."

Cassie dropped back without looking, and ended up just perched on the end of the bed. She hadn't let her fingers out of herself, and they soon started moving again. "Oh, that's good. Not as good as you, but.... Good." She dropped back to lie on the bed.

"I'm being selfish." Cassie said to the ceiling. "I should let you see what I'm doing, shouldn't I?" She couldn't pull her right hand from its rotation in and around her pussy, so she clumsily pushed her knickers down with her left. Somehow, she got them to her knees, then let them slide down to the floor.

Spreading her legs, Cassie gave the camera a view of the fingers working her up to her next orgasm. Two of them pushed in and out, then, occasionally, she stopped to rotate them around her clit and mons.

Maybe her hand was blocking the camera's view of her pussy, she thought. It took a lot of effort, but she pulled her fingers out, slowly and sensually, then moved them up to press at her mons just above the hood of her clitoris. She imagined what she was showing now. Her lips were open, she could feel them, pouting at the lens. The knowledge that the glass eye was taking it all in was enough to push her on toward another, bigger and better, orgasm.

Her clitoris had pushed out past the sheath it normally hid behind. It demanded attention, even though Cassie knew it might be more than she could take. Her circling fingers moved lower, moving the sheath on her clit and making her butt and hips twitch in time. Still slick with her own juices, they slid over the sensitive little bud and she squealed.

The sensations were intense, incredible, almost too much. She wanted to experience them again. She flicked her fingers over her clit, squeaking and jerking as she did. Again and again she did it, until it was too much and she had to stop.

The intense stimulation had left Cassie right on the edge of orgasm. Sitting up again, she pushed three fingers into herself, as far as they would go. She ground against them, thrusting them in and out faster and faster and letting out mounting cries of joy. Her climax was building and building.

Cassie came, pure pleasure pulsing out from her crotch and setting off lights behind her eyes. She was so caught up in the ecstasy of the moment that she slipped off the bed, to curl up on the floor in a panting, sighing heap.

When she had recovered enough, Cassie struggled to her feet and walked over to turn the camera off. "I hope you enjoy watching the show as much as I enjoyed making it." she said as she picked it up to put back in its box.

* * *

NOEL HAD A HUGE GRIN when he opened the door to his flat. He didn't have a chance to say hello before Cassie had wrapped her arms around his neck and pulled him down for a kiss. His hands went down to clasp her buttocks through her jeans and pull her to him. He lifted her until she was on tiptoe, grinding her crotch against his.

Their tongues played against each other as they shuffled through the door. Cassie kicked it closed, then leaned back against it. "Miss me? Why am I asking? I can feel it." She squeezed the erection that was pressing out the material of Noel's trousers. She nodded toward the bedroom.

"I'd love to, but I ordered food for us. It should be here any time now."

"How did you know what to get me?"

"The Golden Moon's set menu for two. You liked it last time."

"Oh, okay, you're forgiven."

"I was going to make something special, but then I realised it would mean spending time in the kitchen when I could be spending it in you."

"In me?"

"With you...?"

"No, in me is good. I like that idea."

The buzzer rang as someone at the house's front door pressed the button for the flat. "Perfect timing." said Noel.

* * *

"I'M STUFFED. I DON'T think I can move." Cassie lay back on the sofa and rubbed her belly. Then she pouted. "I had planned to have lots of sex tonight. Now you've gone and fed me and.... What's the rule? No heavy exercise for an hour after you've eaten?"

"Damn. Another plan I hadn't thought through." Noel nuzzled Cassie's neck and nibbled her earlobe. She made a happy sound. "So, are you all ready for Japan." he asked.

"I think so. This time next week I'll be in a plane...."

"I'm going to miss you. And I'm going to be really jealous. I'd love to go to Japan, even if I did have to work once I got there."

Cassie laid her head on Noel's shoulder. "If they send me again, and they probably will, you should come with me."

"I'll start saving." Noel turned Cassie's head until she faced him, then gently kissed her. She responded, and they lost themselves for a few minutes.

Noel managed to undo the buttons on Cassie's top and his hand found its way into it so he could cup a breast through her bra. She pushed his T-shirt up so that she could play with the hair on his chest.

"Nope, I'm still not up to anything strenuous." Cassie said when their lips parted.

"We have all weekend," Noel reassured her, "and any night next week you want."

"And then I'm going to Japan for four weeks."

"Yeah. But.... you've got a laptop with a web cam on it, haven't you?"

"Yes."

"Well, I thought we could video call. You should have good bandwidth, so it ought to work."

"And you thought we could...."

"Yeah."

"Web cam sex. I wish I'd thought of that. Erm, I did have an idea as well. Not the same, but similar. I tried out the video on my new camera last night, and I shot something to help you remember me while I'm away." Cassie realised she was blushing, though a lot of it was from the warmth spreading out from her groin as she remembered making the video. "It was supposed to be for when I'd gone, but, well, we could watch it now."

Cassie rummaged in her bag and found her camera. "I'm expecting you to have the right cable to plug this into your TV." She said.

"I wouldn't be much of a semi-pro video maker if I didn't, would I?"

It took Noel a couple of minutes to track down the right cable. When the camera was plugged in, he noticed that Cassie looked nervous. "If you don't want me to see this...."

"I want you to, I really do. But I just thought, well, like you said, you shoot video for a living. Part of your living, anyway. What if this is awful? What if I've made a really shit sex tape?"

Noel pondered this. "It's got you in it, with no clothes on?"

"Yes."

"Sounds perfect to me."

"Flatterer." Cassie patted the cushion next to her. "If I get really embarrassed I might have to bury my face in your lap."

"Sounds promising."

Cassie hadn't thought that she would watch her performance. She had a strange relationship with the woman on screen- detached, because she was watching her, and deeply involved, because she remembered each of the touches. It turned her on. If Noel was half as excited by it as she was it had worked.

Unable to take her eyes off the woman on screen, Cassie squirmed in her seat. She remembered promising Noel a blow job as he watched, but was too rapt to follow up. So she reached across and found the outline of his hard on in his trousers. Following its directions, she blindly worked her way up to the belt and fought, one handed, to release it.

Noel helped Cassie release his belt with his left hand whilst his right copied hers and found its way to the front of her jeans. It was easier for him to unbutton her jeans than for her to unzip him, and his strong fingers were soon teasing across the material at the front of her panties.

After fighting with the flap on the front of Noel's boxers, Cassie had his lovely erection in her hand. It was long and thick and topped by a deep red, bulbous head. Cassie loved to look at it, but right now, she was more interested in what the woman on the screen might do next. She grasped the beautiful cock lightly and slowly stroked up and down it.

On screen, Cassie dipped her fingers under the hem of her knickers and into her wet, waiting pussy. Noel's fingers followed her lead, and Cassie let out a little happy sound.

Neither of them could take their eyes off the action on screen. They stroked and penetrated each other as they watched the woman they both knew pleasure herself. Their rhythms sped up and slowed down to match hers, until she climaxed with a wild cry and fell off her bed.

Cassie was very close to coming, but when she looked at Noel, she knew he was even closer. Sliding down his body, she licked her lips and kissed the head of his hard on. It twitched at the attention. Cassie ran her tongue around the warm bulb, wetting it so that she could slide her lips down it

Noel's fingers pushed into Cassie, rolling around and urging her not to stop. She drew back, then dipped her head to take more of him into her. The power she had over him was incredible, and made her so hot. She ran her tongue over the sensitive glans and he shivered.

A glance at the television let Cassie see a close up of her own face, staring at her with wonder. The feeling that she was being watched pushed her over the edge. As she came, her pussy pulsed against Noel's fingers.

She felt the twitch where she held Noel's cock, then tasted his semen as it hit her tongue. She let it fill her mouth, then sucked it down. With a theatrical slurp, she cleaned the glans with her tongue, raising shivers and gasps from Noel.

A last little dribble of cum welled up from the slit at the tip of Noel's cock. Cassie licked it off gently, and he gasped. He was so sensitive just after he came, it was almost evil to tease him like that. She kissed along Noel's length, gently as she let his still hard cock lay down.

Noel's fingers were still inside Cassie, gently moving in little circles. She squirmed under the attention, pulling herself up to kiss his neck and chin. The aftershock of another orgasm rattled through her. Before another one started to well up, she laid her hand over Noel's, squeezing it, but urging him to stop.

The Cassie from the night before was still staring out of the television at them, waiting to see what they did next. "That was hot." Noel said. "You are hot, and that was one dirty, dirty video."

"You enjoyed it then?"

"Oh hell, yeah."

"I enjoyed making it."

"That was obvious."

"You're the expert, was there anything technically wrong with it?"

Noel didn't answer right away, he was obviously weighing up Cassie's likely response to what he had to say. "There was, wasn't there? What was wrong with it?" she said.

"The only thing really wrong with it was it was too dark."

"Oh. Right. I did notice that, a little. What else was wrong?"

"Again, nothing you could really do anything about, but the camera was static, so sometimes you strayed out of shot a bit."

"Maybe I should get one of those selfie sticks for the next one."

"Or maybe," Noel leant forward to whisper conspiratorially, "you need to have a camera man."

"Really?"

"I have a few cameras in the flat, my own and the ones we use for the business. If we filmed tomorrow at the right time, we could have a decent amount of light."

"Would you direct me as well?"

"Maybe. Or you could just do whatever comes naturally. Getting filmed really does turn you on, doesn't it?"

"I didn't expect it to. It's the thought of being watched, I think."

"I will happily watch you."

They kissed. Cassie reached across and stroked Noel's cock, feeling it growing again. She let it go so she could fumble in her bag until she found the box of condoms she had put in, just in case. The kiss broke off, and she showed Noel the box. "Be gentle with me," she said, "the meal's still not completely settled."

✳ ✳ ✳

CASSIE LOOKED OUT OF the window that stretched the width of one wall of the bedroom. "Are you sure nobody can see us?" The curtains had been tied back to keep them open and let in the most light. The thought of someone catching a glance of what they were doing made her nervous, but sent a thrill through her as well.

"We're on the second floor, we'll be fine. No one's going to be able to see in here."

Noel had turned the room into a little studio. There were reflectors against the wall opposite the window, to make the most of the light and fill in shadows, and two cameras on tripods pointed at the bed. One camera was to the right of the foot of the bed, the other was looking across it from just in front of the window. Looking again at the scrolled tubing of the bed head, Cassie confirmed that she had seen an action camera fastened to it. The last piece of kit was a digital SLR in a strange circular frame- to make it a sort of steady cam, Noel had said- which was sat on its own stand at the foot of the bed. All of this is going to be pointing at me, Cassie thought, tingling at the exciting prospect. "Don't you have any more cameras?" She said, grinning.

"You don't want to know the answer to that."

"What's that ring on the front of the camera?" Cassie pointed.

"Circular light around the lens. I use it to light smaller stuff when I'm taking close ups. I thought it would make a good pussy light."

"Pussy light?"

"Technical term."

"You've done this before haven't you?"

"Not this, nothing this cool. I took a glamour photography course once, though."

"I don't have the boobs for glamour photos."

"No, your tits are way better. We can start whenever you're ready. I just need to press record on all these cameras."

Cassie was wearing Noel's bath robe, ready to reveal the sexy underwear she had chosen as soon as she slipped it off. She tapped her lips, as if deep in thought. "There's one last thing, I think. Take your clothes off."

Noel was naked in moments. He stood facing Cassie, his cock already half hard and sticking out in front of him. That was how a good cameraman should be, Cassie thought. "You'd best start the cameras." she said.

As Noel moved quickly around the bed, Cassie let the robe drop to the floor. The thong she wore was little more than a triangle of material joined by thick string which was tied in a bow at either side like bikini bottoms. Her bra was made of a gauzy material so that her areolae and already stiff nipples were as good as on show. The cups lifted her breasts up and pushed them out, making them even perkier than normal. Noel stopped by the SLR when he saw her outfit, and gave her an appreciative look up and down. "Nice. Get on the bed when you're ready." He picked up the camera, pointed it at Cassie and pressed record. "And I'll make you a star."

Cassie felt the same warmth spreading through her as the night before. Noel was watching her now, recording her, and probably joining in. But he'd be watching it by himself later and, maybe, one day they might show the final version to others. All those eyes she could imagine looking at her, enjoying her body, being turned on by her. She gave a little bow and blew a kiss at the camera before climbing onto the bed.

Kneeling on the bed, Cassie looked around at all the lenses looking at her. All the attention, from every side, made her wet. "What should I do?" she asked, suddenly at a loss.

"Show us what you've got." Noel was crouched at the foot of the bed, shooting Cassie from a low angle, constantly checking the view on the camera's little screen.

"I can do that." Cassie leaned forward, letting Noel's camera get a shot of her cleavage. "You like the view? Of course you do. But that little camera back there is going to get a really naughty view." She reached back with her right hand to move the string of her thong to one side, then part her butt cheeks. She didn't look back, just hoped that the little camera on the bed head had a clear view of the hole she flashed at it.

Bringing her hand back, Cassie prowled down the bed on all fours, until she was at the end, up close to Noel and his camera. She licked her lips, and took a quick look down. Just as she had thought, he was very, very hard. "Why don't you bring that up here?" she whispered.

Noel stood slowly, keeping the camera focused on her face as he did. When he was upright, his hard on came into the shot. Cassie reached out to pull it toward her mouth, though it was so stiff she almost couldn't. She slid her lips over the head a few times, then ran her tongue down the shaft. Noel must be having a tough time keeping his camera steady. To make it worse for him, Cassie backed away and let his erection go.

Stretching out on the bed, Cassie grinned up at Noel. He was flushed with excitement at the truncated blow job, but managed to hold the camera stable. After a moment to draw a slow breath, he zoomed in and panned down her body as she took hold of the bed head and rotated her hips. He zoomed out again and took a step back.

Cassie looked down the length of her body at Noel's erection, standing proud and aroused and all but throbbing. She spread her legs, giving him something more to focus on, and brought her hands down to her breasts. Her nipples were hard and long, poking hard against the material of her bra. She squeezed each tender tip between thumb and forefinger and squeaked.

The bra was front fastening, so Cassie reached down and released the clasp. She didn't move the cups aside, though, moving her fingers down her body until they reached the bows on the sides of her thong. She pulled the ends of the bows and released them, but she didn't move the material away.

One false move away from exposing herself, Cassie moved her legs even wider and stretched her arms out. She could feel the flush of her skin as the bra cups balanced on her nipples, waiting to fall off. Noel crouched down again and moved around to get a different angle.

Running her right forefinger down a bra strap, Cassie lifted, and then gently pushed aside, the right bra cup. Noel zoomed in on the exposed breast, his breath speeding up as things hotted up again. Cassie ran a finger around the nipple, then slid it across to the other breast to push that cup off. Propping herself on her elbows, she let the bra straps slide down her arms and then off, putting it to one side.

Noel was staring at her over the top of his camera, desire evident in just the set of his brow. She stared back at him, reading just how much he wanted her right now, and felt the heat grow between her legs. She could have given in to the urge and pulled him toward her, but the longer they built it up, the greater it would be when their bodies met again.

Cassie reached down her body until she found the strings from the front of her thong. She pinched them each between a thumb and forefinger and started slowly drawing them up. Noel was back at the foot of the bed, the camera perched on the sheet and watching the reveal in close up.

The triangle of material pulled up and away from Cassie's crotch, revealing the outer edges of her labia, puffed up and excited. Then the string caught where it was trapped under her body and tautened, pulling the scrap of material between her pussy lips. She could tell by the silence as Noel held his breath that the effect was sexy to him.

Slowly, the material, and then the string, of the thong pulled between Cassie's lips as she tugged some more. Eventually, she could put the little wisp of material aside and lie there naked for Noel to look down at her. She watched as he panned up her legs, paused at her crotch and neatly trimmed bush, then carried on the shot upwards. When he was focussed on her face she stared back at him through the lens. Not taking her eyes from the camera, she brought her right hand up and sucked the first two fingers into her mouth. Moving them in and out, she got them nice and wet.

Noel followed the fingers as Cassie moved them down to her crotch. They traced a line down her labia, feeling the warmth and slickness there, then she spread her legs and scissored her fingers to open herself to his view. This was an intimate move, even with her lover, and to be getting it on video felt deliciously dirty. She slid both fingers in, keeping them as far apart as she could.

Cassie pressed her hand back against her mons. With her fingers spread, they framed her clitoris, which had popped out, pink and sensitive, to join in the fun. She moved her fingers in and out, to savour the sensation of their short thrusts and their contact with her sensitive bud.

The camera was focussed on Cassie's fingers as they moved in and out, but Noel was looking over it, along her body and at her face. Through half closed eyes she saw him, a happy, horny expression on his flushed face, and knew she needed some help from him. "Give me the camera." she whispered, reaching out with her free hand.

Noel handed the camera to Cassie and she took hold of the rig one handed. Resting it one her chest, she managed to turn it until it pointed back down her body, framing both the motion of her hands and the magnificent curve of Noel's erection. Reluctantly, she removed her fingers from her pussy so that she could hold the camera in both hands. Lifting it to focus on Noel's face, she said, "I need you to lick me."

With a huge grin, Noel bent over to comply. He planted his hands just inside Cassie's knees, so that he could lift them and spread them later. His mouth hovered over her waiting lips, and she arched her hips up toward it. Still he teased, never quite letting her make contact.

Cassie watched Noel on the camera's screen, as if he was far away, maybe even doing this to someone else. But she could feel the warmth of his skin against her thighs, even feel his breath on her crotch. It was hard to hold the camera still and keep him in shot.

Finally, Noel's tongue sneaked out. It traced up the crease at the top of Cassie's thigh, teasingly, terribly close to her labia, but oh so far away at the same time. She trembled, waiting. Her hands gripped the camera rig so tight the knuckles were white. The tip of the tongue traced up the inside of one thigh and then the other. If her hands hadn't been full, she would have reached out and grasped the back of his head to push him down where she needed him.

Lips pursed around Cassie's clit, not quite touching it, but enclosing it in warmth. She fought to stay calm and still, to keep the camera aimed at the action. But this became less and less easy as the lips closed, embracing the sensitive nub, then sliding up and down it like it was a tiny penis. She hadn't realised just how long it could become, how far it had poked out. She squealed. The sensation was intense, almost too intense, and it coursed all through her.

"Too much." Cassie gasped. "Don't stop." The camera slipped from her grasp and got a close up shot of the bed.

Noel did stop. The tip of his tongue flicked around the edges of Cassie's clit, but didn't touch it again. He clasped his arms around her thighs to hold her as she writhed under him, then ran his tongue from the bottom to the top of her slit.

Kissing along her right thigh to her knee, Noel released his grip on Cassie. He reached over and picked up the camera, smiling at her as he spotted her following her movements. With his left hand he held the camera, whilst his right slid down her thigh until it teased the skin close to her pussy. Cassie held still, waiting for him to go further, certain that he would tease her more should she reach out for his hand.

Cassie's sex pouted, the slick, engorged lips parting and inviting Noel's fingers in. She looked at his face as he studied the sight, awe and arousal in his expression. Biting her lower lip, she waited.

Gently, two fingers entered Cassie, sliding in easily on the lubrication from Noel's tongue and her own excitement. She opened up to them, felt them exploring her. When he started pumping them in and out of her, she allowed herself to move again, responding to the way they caressed her insides.

Noel slowed the fingers moving inside Cassie. It was still exquisite, but she wanted to make a low sound of complaint. Before she could, he had twisted his fingers around and crooked them so that the tips rubbed against the front wall of her vagina. They found the rough bit, the bundle of nerves that were oh so sensitive, and massaged it.

Cassie had dug her heels in and lifted her hips to arch her back so that she curved up to meet the attention of those fingers. Noel had crooked his left arm around and was holding the camera on his shoulder so it could look down on what he was doing to her. The ring of lights around the lens- the pussy light- was on, its gentle glow illuminating the action of his fingers as they thrust and ground inside her.

"Fuck me. I need you in me." Cassie said. She was so close to coming that her body didn't want Noel to stop, even for a moment. But her heart wanted him in her.

Noel pulled his fingers from Cassie, and she drifted back down to the bed. He put the camera down and came round to kiss Cassie as he rolled the condom down his erection. "Roll over." he said when he was ready. "Get on all fours."

When Cassie was on all fours facing the bed head, Noel put the camera under her, angling it up so that it lit and was filming her crotch. Another intimate angle exposed. Cassie spread her legs a little more. She looked up at the action camera and let it see the passion on her face.

Noel teased Cassie. He ran the head of his cock between the lips of her pussy, then slipped it forward so that the camera got a shot of it against her pubic hair. Pulling back, he took hold of it and aimed it, sliding it between her lips and into the waiting warmth. The action camera got to see Cassie's mouth form a little O as she squeezed Noel's hard cock.

Strong hands grasped Cassie's waist and Noel started moving in and out of her. His fingers had been incredible inside her, but his erection was even better. It was fatter and longer and pressed against her G spot on every thrust in.

Cassie cried out encouragement, and Noel's thrusts became harder and faster. Her body rocked back and forth each time he drove into her. Neither of them knew, or cared, what sort of shots the camera under them was getting.

The audience for this little film they were making would care, Cassie told herself, a little voice in a head full of cries of pleasure. But by now, the audience would be ripe for some fast moving thrusting and a rapidly approaching climax.

The idea of being watched pushed Cassie over the edge. The orgasm developed in the deepest parts of her being reached by Noel's cock and vibrated out, along the length of it and then through her thighs and up her belly to her breasts. She sang out her pleasure. Noel provided rhythm with his grunts, until he, too, called out his orgasm.

They toppled over to the side and snuggled up. Noel picked up the camera and held it at arms length as they kissed and nuzzled. "Wow." Cassie managed after a while. Sex with Noel was always good, but with an audience it was even better.

"Wow's a good word for it." Noel nibbled Cassie's neck.

"I've seen porn. Aren't you supposed to come on my tits or something?"

"We can handle that in the re-shoots."

"Okay mister director. Shouldn't you turn the cameras off until then?"

"In a while. I want to cuddle."

* * *

CASSIE WASN'T SURE where the week had gone. There had been briefings at work, and sex with Noel. Packing her cases, and sex with Noel. Looking at the footage they had shot on Saturday, and sex with Noel so they could shoot more. There had been, she happily remembered, a lot of sex with Noel. They both wanted to have as much intimate time together as possible, to save up and get them through four weeks apart.

Standing in the departures lounge, Cassie looked up at the board. It flashed, and it was time for her to go through for boarding. She turned around to face Noel, who held her carry on satchel.

She didn't want to say anything right now, simply reaching up to wrap her arms around his neck and pull him down for a kiss. He held her around the waist and pulled her in close.

When they parted he said, quietly, "I'm going to miss you."

"I know, me too. At least you have several hours of me to keep you company."

"I do. You'll be my reason to stay in at nights."

There was a pause, drawn out as they looked at each other. "I love you." they both said together, before blushing.

"I've got to go now." Cassie said, happy minutes of kissing later. "Or I'm going to start crying."

"Me too. It would be horribly messy."

"And embarrassing for all these other people." Cassie could feel the moisture at the corner of her eyes. If she carried on joking about crying she'd be bawling in no time. She stood on tiptoe to steal one last quick kiss from Noel, took the satchel from him and then headed for the gate. She gave him a little wave just before disappearing into air side.

Four weeks was going to be a long time without her new lover, but she had a big adventure to look forward to. And they could video call. That had so many wonderfully dirty possibilities.

Cassie Online

Cassie felt like she still had jet-lag. As she had been in Japan for over a week now, it had to be culture overload instead. She wanted to take in everything the country had to offer, but, crashed out on the futon, she had to admit that she'd tried to cram too much into her first week. Her feet ached from the miles she had walked around Tokyo the day before, camera slung under her arm for quick pics and her gaze always up to take in the signs and the neon.

She was going to be in the country for another three weeks. It wouldn't be enough time to see everything she wanted, especially as she was working during the weeks. But she'd have to slow down on the sightseeing if she wanted to stay sane. The other thing that would keep her sane was talking to her man. She checked the little clock on the wall and did a quick calculation. It would still be six in the morning in Britain. He would be logging on and video calling her in four hours. She could probably wait that long.

The apartment they had put her up in was just what she had expected, what she had hoped for. One room, a bathroom and a kitchen that was really just a cupboard with a cooker and sink in it. The sort of place she had seen in hundreds of manga over the years. She could be the alienated college kid plotting, or being caught up in, world changing events, or the lonely and lonesome lovelorn outsider, sighing their life away until a magical girlfriend or boyfriend came along. Most likely the latter, as she was thousands of miles away from friends and family and waiting for the technical magic of a video booty call.

As she was musing about being all alone in a foreign country, it was very strange for there to be a knock at the door. Cassie wondered if she was hearing someone at the next flat. These little boxes were tightly packed, and the walls thin. Two nights earlier, she had been kept awake by the guy upstairs and the woman he had brought home as they went about it with enthusiasm.

There was another knock, and it was definitely at her door. She stood and walked the few steps to answer it.

The woman on Cassie's doorstep was short, gorgeous and, for an embarrassing moment, unrecognisable. She had a lovely round face with brown eyes, tiny nose and thin, dark lips. Her skin was a medium tan and jet black hair fell straight to her shoulders and had a straight cut fringe across her forehead. She just reached Cassie's nose. Her tiny body, emphasised by the cut of her jeans and button down top, was perfect- small breasts and a narrow waist were exactly the right size for a gently flowing outline. She smiled, amused by Cassie's confusion.

"Megumi-san?" Cassie said as recognition struck her. "Hello. What are you doing here?" She managed to ask the question in her clumsy Japanese.

"I am nearly your neighbour. I live in the next block along. When I found your address I thought it would be nice to come and say hello." Megumi's English was almost accent-less. She picked up a bag that had been at her feet and held it out. "I visited my family, and mother always sends me back with too much food. I wondered if you would like to share."

"Oh, yes please. Please come in."

Cassie took the bag as Megumi removed her shoes, then gestured her toward the room. Her unexpected guest looked around with a little smile. "These little boxes are all the same. Oh, but mine does not have a balcony." She opened the tiny door and stepped out. There was just enough room on the balcony for a seat and a small table. The view was of more boxy buildings made up of similar apartments, with just a hazy hint of hills in the distance. Nonetheless, Cassie planned to eat breakfasts there when she was more organised, but had hardly spent any time on it yet. She put the bag down and stood at the door- there wasn't room enough for both of them outside.

"Would you like some tea? Or I have fruit juice."

"English tea?" Megumi stepped back inside.

"I brought some with me. I didn't know whether I could find any here." Cassie realised that she had been speaking half English and half Japanese. It seemed natural.

"Yes please, I would like to try English tea."

As Cassie busied herself in the tiny kitchen- or, more accurately, the hallway by the kitchen cupboard- Megumi took boxes from her bag and put them on the table. "Are you liking Japan? Is this your first visit?" she asked.

"It is. The first of many, I hope. It is very impressive. There is so much to see."

"I still feel that way about Tokyo sometimes, and I moved here a year ago."

"Oh, where did you move from?"

"A small town up in the mountains. I went to University in Kyoto, but it is not as big as Tokyo. So when the chance came, I moved here right away."

Cassie brought the two cups of tea to the table and sat beside Megumi on the futon. Megumi took her cup, sniffed it and then took a sip. She appeared disappointed by the flavour, but took a few more sips to become accustomed to it. "I would really like to visit England one day. Our companies have exchanges that go the other way, so I am trying to get onto one of them."

"England's not as exciting as Tokyo."

"You say that because it is where you grew up. It would be as strange and interesting to me as Japan is to you."

"Well, I will happily show you around, and try to find all the most interesting places."

"That would be lovely. So, I have brought you all this food, because mama-san believes I do not eat properly now I am in the city. It would be my pleasure to share it with you."

"I would be honoured. You will have to tell me what everything is."

＊ ＊ ＊

THEY ATE, AND CHATTED about work, hobbies, pop music and, inevitably, men. Cassie had glanced at the clock on the wall, and realised how long they had been talking. She took the two steps across the floor and picked up her laptop. "My boyfriend will be calling soon." she explained. "I should be online when he logs in."

"Your boyfriend in England? Is he handsome?" When Cassie blushed, Megumi smiled. "He is? And is he, what is the English phrase? Is he well hung?"

"Well, I, er.... Yes, he is." There didn't seem any point in denying it, so Cassie decided to take pride in her lover's endowment.

"And he is nice to you? Obviously he cares enough to call from the other side of the world."

"He is lovely. A real gentleman."

"And a good lover?"

"Yes, he is."

"Aah, you are so lucky. All the men I find are useless. Even the ones with big penises do not know how to use them properly." Megumi said, sighing.

"You just haven't met the right man. How many have you tried?"

"Five.... Six, maybe. I do not think he counts because he couldn't get it up. How many did you have to try before you found your handsome, well hung man?"

"Seven. I mean, he's the seventh. Some of the others were okay, but others were a real disappointment."

"I have toys now. It is so much better than being let down all the time. How long have you been with your handsome man?"

"A month."

"Just a month? Do you miss him? And all the sex you must have been having?"

"I do."

"All my toys take my mind off the sex I am not having."

"I have to admit, I was planning to get something when I got here, but I completely forgot yesterday."

"I know the best places to go. Next week, I shall be your guide, just like you promised to be for me when I visit England."

Cassie couldn't help but laugh. "It's a deal. But not just sex toy shops, I want to see all sorts of places. I want to find the best manga and toys and games and models."

"Are you.... What is the English word for otaku?"

"I think geek comes close."

"I shall take you to all the geek places."

"That's a great idea."

The laptop pinged, and a window opened. Cassie and Megumi leant forward to see what appeared in the little box. An incomplete ring turned and turned, until, eventually, a face appeared. Cassie felt a little flutter in her chest, and a lovely, tight warmth between her legs. "Hello there." she said, grinning.

"Hello." said Noel. He looked back and forth, confused to be seeing two women on his screen.

"Megumi, this is Noel. Noel, Megumi."

Megumi and Noel said their hellos, then Megumi announced, "I shall leave you two now. And I shall see you at work tomorrow, Cassandra-san." When she had picked up her boxes and walked around behind the screen, Megumi leant forward and said in Japanese, "He is very handsome. You were right."

Cassie realised she was blushing. On screen, Noel was looking around, as if trying to find the source of the voice he had just heard. Megumi had a cheeky grin as she skipped down the corridor and pulled on her shoes. Cassie watched until Megumi had let herself out, then turned back to the screen.

"Neighbour?" asked Noel.

"Almost. We work together as well. She looks so different out of office wear."

"So how has your first week been?"

"Hectic. And awesome. I could go on and on about it all for hours."

"Well, I've got all day, go ahead."

So she did. Noel watched, with a grin, as Cassie described the office she was working in, the commute, her one room flat and how she was coping with cooking instructions she only half understood. She became particularly animated as she described her journey around Tokyo the day before, exhausting herself as she took in too much of the city in one go. He hardly had to say a word for over an hour. Eventually, she started punctuating sentences with yawns. "You should get some sleep." Noel suggested.

"But you haven't told me your news."

"I don't really have any news. I'm getting a van. It's a bit rough, but I can get bigger things back from auctions than in Steve's car."

"You can put a mattress in the back and we can drive out to the countryside."

"I like that idea."

Cassie yawned extravagantly before she could form her next sentence. "You definitely need some sleep." Noel told her.

"Okay. Send me pictures of the shag wagon when you get it."

"I will. Bye." Noel's picture disappeared.

Cassie could just manage to reach across to the laptop to shut it down. Slowly, socks shuffling across the floor, she did her evening routine. A couple of steps at a time took her from folding the futon out into a bed to pulling the curtains, putting washing in the sink, locking the door and brushing her teeth. She stripped slowly and clumsily, dropping clothes on the floor, until she was naked. Somewhere, she had pyjamas, but she couldn't be bothered to look for them.

Wrapped in the sheets, Cassie remembered that she and Noel had planned to tease each other and make love over the video link. She had been too tired, and too full of news, to even think about it. Recalling the plan, Cassie was washed over with the warmth of a lazy arousal. She wished she didn't, because it would feel like cheating to come now, when she should have done it whilst Noel could watch.

Cassie slipped into sleep, and dreamt strange and erotic dreams about wandering around neon-lit Tokyo streets in the nude, trying to track down her lover.

✻ ✻ ✻

CASSIE CHECKED HER personal emails at lunch, whilst she and Megumi ate at the desk. They had started doing this the week before, as a way for Cassie to hone her conversational Japanese. "Is that message from your boyfriend?" Megumi asked. "You said his name was Noel."

Looking at the time stamp, Noel had sent the message shortly after their conversation the night before. Yesterday morning for him, she remembered. "I talked and talked and talked at him last night. This is probably the only way he could think of to get a word in. Let's see what he's got to say."

'Lights, camera, action!' the subject line read. Cassie clicked on it without thinking, then reddened as she realised what it was about.

Megumi had leant in for a look, she couldn't help being nosey. "I forgot to say, but the film is ready and uploaded. Hope you enjoy watching it as much as I did editing it." she read. "I am sorry, I should not be such a snoop. But I am intrigued. He has made a film?"

"We made a film. Together."

"What sort of.... Oh." Megumi's voice dropped to a whisper, "You made a.... sex film?"

Cassie nodded, strangely proud, both of making the film with Noel and of admitting to it. But she went bright red when Megumi asked, "Can I watch it?"

When she was able to speak again, Cassie couldn't form her reply in Japanese, "I haven't seen it yet. But, you know what? I'll ask my co-star, and if he's okay with it, then yes, you can."

Megumi grinned and almost bounced in her chair with excitement. "Oh, we are such a naughty pair aren't we? Who would believe my co-worker makes naughty films?"

"Let's keep it a secret, okay?"

"Of course. If I cannot keep a secret, I do not deserve to see your film."

✳ ✳ ✳

THERE WAS A SMALL STORE at the end of the road Cassie's building was on. The vending machine outside sold phone charms, small, cartoony creatures on short nylon loops which could be attached to a mobile to add cuteness. Cassie had started collecting them, and was going to make a kawaii necklace when she had enough to string together.

Inside, the shop reminded Cassie of the type of corner shop that was becoming so rare in Britain, only, if anything, more tightly packed and with a wider range of merchandise. The middle aged lady who ran the shop had been so surprised that a blue eyed blonde girl would talk to her in Japanese that she happily let Cassie stumble through conversations where she asked the proper names of the things she bought.

Having described what she was looking for, Cassie now had the ingredients to attempt a recreation of the tofu salad which had been one of the dishes Megumi had brought the day before. She set her laptop downloading the video as she prepared everything on the tiny worktop.

The video was still downloading when Cassie sat down with her meal. It finished loading whilst she ate, but she put off watching it, clearing away the meal, having a shower and putting on pyjamas before she sat down before the computer again.

She had promised herself that she would not masturbate unless Noel was on the other end of a video chat to watch her, and, hopefully, join in. It was going to be hard to watch this video and keep to her vow. She stared at the icon for a long time, before leaning forward to click on it and set the playback off.

The video faded up from black, and Cassie was looking at herself from just over two weeks before. She stood in Noel's bedroom, wearing sexy underwear, posed for a while, then climbed onto the bed and started teasing the cameraman.

Noel had set up several cameras around the bed to capture the action, and the video cut to different views as Cassie started playing with herself. She remembered cheekily trying to flash her bum hole at one of the cameras, but still flushed when she saw the image it had captured.

Cassie remembered the feelings of the session when they had shot the video. She could all but taste Noel's cock, and feel its warm head, as the version of her on screen kissed it and teased him with little licks. Her nipples hardened and rubbed against the cotton of her pyjama top as she watched herself teasingly remove her bra and then, so slowly, pull the thong between her pussy lips.

Pressing her legs together, to keep a creeping hand at bay, Cassie squirmed on the futon. She was teasing herself, torturing, almost, watching this video of her own sexual ecstasy and refusing to touch herself. There was a warmth in her groin, she knew she would be so wet down there if she just tested it with a finger. Her legs stayed resolutely pressed together.

On screen Cassie was pleasuring herself, squeaking with intense joy every time her fingers teased at her clit. On the futon, Cassie felt sympathetic spikes of joy from her clitoris as it remembered those touches. The pleasure washed out from the little nub and warmed her whole body. If she came just from watching the video- without touching herself- did that count as not breaking her own rules?

Then Noel joined on screen Cassie on the bed, and went down on her. Cassie knew she could come now, just from watching the rest of the video. The couple she watched were gorgeous and eager to please each other. She felt no shame in her opinion The version of herself she was watching was incredibly sexy, confident and in control. It felt strange to admit that she loved this version of herself. This was the Cassie she wanted to project to the world.

Megumi might watch this, Cassie thought. No, Megumi had to watch this, she decided. Somebody had to see how much she loved Noel, and how wonderful the physical expression of that love could be, and the beautiful woman she worked with was the ideal person. Noel could be convinced, she was sure.

Cassie tried to picture Megumi as she watched the video. Would she be naked, fully clothed, or somewhere in between? At work, she tended to wear long, navy blue skirts and shapeless blouses that hid her lovely body. For a moment, Cassie could just imagine Megumi sitting back on a futon just like this one, half the buttons of her blouse undone to reveal the cups of her bra. She'd hitch her left leg up onto the cushions, then draw the skirt up and reach down to finger herself through her panties.

Or perhaps she would be naked. Cassie recalled the lines of Megumi's body, as revealed by her tight clothes the day before. She could imagine a slim body, with firm, perky breasts and shapely legs. There would be a small patch of deep black pubic hair between her legs. She would play with it a little before reaching down and sliding a finger between her pussy lips just as she watched Noel slide into Cassie on screen.

Cassie climaxed. It was a strange, diffuse orgasm that flushed the skin all over her body, all the way from toes to scalp, making it feel like it was glowing with the pleasure. Little after shocks of pleasure pulsed out from her crotch. She wrapped her arms around her legs and hugged them to her body as the little shivers dissipated, watching the end of the film in soft focus.

Smiling at the warm afterglow, Cassie felt a little smug. She had kept her promise to herself, which had needed a lot of self control, yet still experienced the pleasure rush of an orgasm. She had also, she realised, had sexual thoughts about another woman for the first time. She supposed she should feel confused about this, but she didn't. Megumi was gorgeous, and their fast friendship had reached a level of intimate secret sharing she hadn't enjoyed since the early days of university.

It was perfectly natural for Cassie to imagine Megumi watching the video she had made with Noel. Of course the other woman would be excited by it- Cassie had participated, and she had been turned on by it. She might have resisted the urge to touch herself, but Megumi wouldn't hold herself back. If the slim Japanese beauty had been beside her on the futon, Cassie would have reached across and run her hands up her shapely legs until they met, then slid her fingers along the warm wet lips of her pussy, slowly pushing them inside....

Cassie felt the warmth growing again between her legs. Her erotic reverie was turning her on again, and she might not be able to resist touching herself this time. Plus, if she carried on thinking such things, how was she ever going to talk to Megumi at work without going deep red. She sat up and lifted the computer onto her lap so that she could compose a message telling Noel what a great job he had done editing their little sex tape together. If she could work in a hint about letting Megumi see it, that would be good as well.

* * *

THIS TIME, CASSIE WAS properly prepared for her call from Noel. She stared at the laptop, willing him to call. When that didn't work, she checked her outfit, wanting his first view of it to be just right.

It was a Japanese schoolgirl cosplay outfit. Cassie had opted for the navy blue type, rather than the ones with tartan skirts. The pleated skirt was short enough that she'd have been sent home if it had ever been part of her school uniform. With her feet planted on the table either side of the laptop, she had to push the front of the skirt down to keep from flashing her plain white panties. The blouse was cut tighter than a school uniform would have allowed, as well, and the white wing collars were open far enough down to reveal cleavage and the edges of her bra. Her hair was too short for pigtails, so she had brushed it all forward to give herself and exaggerated fringe. The outfit was completed by flat pumps and white leg warmers which were bunched up so that they reached no higher than her knees.

The outfit felt silly, but in the best possible way. It was a self-conscious tease and a deliberate play on sexy stereotypes. She hoped Noel liked it, though she didn't plan to be wearing it for the whole of his call. In a box beside her on the futon, Cassie had arranged some of the other things she had bought in Akihabara the day before. She was doing inventory on them when the laptop made its incoming message sound.

"Hel-low." Noel said, the end of the word stretching out, full of innuendo.

Cassie blew a kiss at the screen. "You know what we forgot to do last week?"

"Oh, yeah. That was silly of us, wasn't it?"

"Well, there was no way I was going to pass on it this week. Not after you sent that video over. What do you think of the outfit?"

"Very naughty. Very sexy. Have you been looking at my comic collection?"

"I haven't, yet. But I will be when I get back. Megumi-san took me out and showed me the biggest sex shop ever. I got this and some toys." Cassie leaned forward to confide, "They gave me a discount because I let them take a picture and put it on their wall."

"Oooh, I bet you enjoyed that, my gorgeous exhibitionist."

Cassie imagined all the people looking at the picture of her posing in her sexy uniform, lifting the hem of the already short skirt to reveal even more thigh. She had a little shiver run through her body. "Megumi says she has some very naughty outfits of her own."

"Well, if she wants to watch our film, maybe she should show us some of them."

"So, you're okay with letting her see it?"

"Oh yes, definitely. I love the idea of someone else watching what we did. And I know the thought of being watched turns you on. Anything that turns you on, turns me on."

"I love you, you know."

"I know."

"I.... don't think I'll give her the film until I'm going to leave. I mightn't be able to sit still at work knowing that she'd seen it."

"Okay." Noel said, through a snort of laughter.

"Are you in your bedroom?"

"I am."

"Using your tablet?"

"Yes."

"Is it waterproof?"

Noel was confused by the question. "I think so. Well, splash-proof, anyway."

"Good, good. Would you like to see what else I bought?"

"Yes please."

"Well, I picked up a web cam with a really long cable and a light on it." Cassie reached out and picked the camera from where it was attached to the laptop screen. "So that you can see what's going on when I do things like this."

She turned the little light on and slowly moved it up her left leg and under the hem of her skirt. Noel's expression as he got a close up of her knickers was priceless.

"I like that. Where else could you put it, I wonder?"

"I'll find lots of places, I'm sure. But let's have a look at some of my other toys first." Cassie put the web cam down on the table, moving it until the little inset box on the screen had the image she wanted in it. Planting her feet back on the floor, she sat back with her legs open and folded the skirt up to reveal her panties to the light.

Noel's expression was wonderful. He was gently biting his lower lip, and leaning in to get a better view of the picture on his tablet's screen. Cassie ran a finger over the material of her panties, tracing the lines of the lips beneath them. When she had furrowed out the impression of her pussy, she reached into the box and picked up the cutest of the toys she had bought the day before.

It looked like a larger version of the phone charms she had been collecting, a green cartoony creature with a large head atop a body of about the same size. Just big enough to fill the palm of her, it had two bulges on top which were painted with big eyes, and a big, smiling swash of a mouth. She turned it over and there were little raised nubs on the bottom. Holding it up to the camera, she flicked the switch on the back and it started buzzing.

The little toy's body was vibrating, the camera's microphone picked up the buzz of the motor. "Now then, what are you going to do with that?" Noel asked.

"Just you watch." Cassie brought the vibrator up to the front of her panties and hovered it over the furrow she had just made, not quite touching, but close enough that she was sure she could feel its motion. She moved it around over the material, sensing where it was all the time, until she could hold back no more and had to press it against herself. She moved the vibrator until it touched the waistband of her panties, thrilling to the buzz of it.

Cassie glanced up to see Noel watching her, his expression full of lust and anticipation. She ran the little toy along the waistband, then traced little sweeps across the front panel, teasingly keeping them away from the edges of her pussy lips.

The material of her underwear had to be soaking, Cassie thought, she was so turned on by the gentle vibration and playing to an audience. She brought the vibrator over to stimulate her clitoris through the cotton of her panties, and found her hips jerking up to press harder against the toy.

If she carried on running the vibrator around her most sensitive parts, Cassie knew she would come in moments. But she didn't want to do that, she needed to draw this out as long as possible. Turning it off, she put the toy aside. "I want to see your cock." she said.

Noel was eager to oblige. The view from his end bounced around a bit as he worked out how to comply, then Cassie found she was looking at the ceiling of his room. He came into view, kneeling over the tablet and foreshortened in an exaggerated way. He was wearing the baggy climbing trousers he liked to lounge around in and, revealed as he pushed them down his legs, nothing underneath. His hard cock filled the screen of Cassie's laptop.

In other circumstances, the image could have been amusing or ludicrous, but Cassie was turned on by it. "Stroke it." she commanded, and watched as Noel's fingers closed around the shaft and started moving up and down it slowly. She wanted to kiss it, but it was thousands of miles away. She would have to settle for what she had in her box.

But first, she should match Noel's exposure. Putting the little vibrator aside, Cassie hooked her thumbs into the waistband of her panties and pushed them down her legs. She looked at the image in the inset box on screen to make sure she was showing off her red, slick lips to best effect. She parted the deep pink labia with her fingers to show Noel just how wet she was, then reached into the box for her next toy.

What she pulled out wasn't the toy she had been aiming for. She hadn't been sure whether she would use it or not, but now that it was out, she wasn't going to put it back.

Holding the purple butt plug up to the camera, Cassie announced, "Look what I've got here. I've only used one of these a couple of times, but I want to share this time with you."

Only the dark red head of Noel's cock could be seen on screen now, he had leaned forward to get a better look at the toy Cassie held up. He grinned, and the smile had a very dirty and sexy edge.

Cassie turned around so that she was on her knees facing the futon, her backside pointing at the web cam. It was hard to look around and check what was on the screen, but the knowledge of how she was exposing her most intimate parts provided plenty of excitement by itself.

"If you're really good, you'll get to go where this is going." Cassie said, absently, as she swirled lube around the butt plug's tip. When she was sure it was slick enough, she reached back with it.

She really only had done this a couple of times before. Some feeling of shame that she no longer had had kept her from experimenting with anal play beyond a few times. But now she was ready to give it another go.

Twisting and trying to look back at the image on her computer's screen, Cassie could see what she was doing. Somehow, it made the exercise trickier. She stopped trying to aim by sight and opted for feel. The tip of the plug pressed against the crease between her butt cheeks, just above the puckered entrance she was aiming for. She brought it down until she felt the end lodge in the ring of muscle.

Relax, Cassie told herself. She had to relax and slowly push the butt plug in. This way, the stiff toy began to enter her. It felt so wrong to be pushing something up there, in the best possible way. She spread around it, opened for it, as its diameter grew. Her confidence faltered for a moment, was she going to be able to take it all in?

At the same time as she started to have doubts, the widest part of the plug passed the ring of muscle. Beyond that point, it narrowed again, before flaring sharply out top form a base. It was like she sucked in the last section of it as it lodged into place. It was a surprise, and Cassie let out a little gasp at the delicious, dirty feeling of the plug in her back passage.

"Woah." said Noel.

Cassie reached back until she found the web cam, then brought it up to smile into the lens. "You bring out the dirtiest part of me." she said. "Want a close up?"

"Yeah." said Noel, his voice strangled.

Moving around so that she could better see the screen of her computer, Cassie moved the little camera down until it had a good view of the base of the butt plug where it stuck out of her. She tensed her muscles, and made the base move a short distance up and down.

"Fuck." said Noel. He was normally so eloquent, the show was definitely working.

Cassie moved the camera down, so that it showed Noel the wet lips of her sex. "I need to put something in there next. Then I want to see if we can come together even though we're so far apart." she said.

Moving carefully, she placed the camera back on the table, then climbed onto the futon facing the computer. With her feet flat on the floor and her butt on the edge, she exposed the end of the butt plug and the lips of her pussy to the camera. Time to complete the show. She leant back against the cushions, and started unbuttoning her blouse. When it was open, she released the fastener on the front of her bra and pushed the cups off her breasts. "Show me your cock again." she ordered.

Noel's magnificent erection came into view again. It was possible it was bigger, it was definitely a deeper shade of red. He was stroking it as slowly as his self control would allow. Cassie reached into the box and pulled out the surrogate she would have to settle for.

The dildo wasn't rigid, drooping slightly from where Cassie's hand grasped it and, whilst realistically sized and sculpted, was unnaturally clear. She brought it up to her lips and kissed the head, then took some of its length into her mouth. She moved it in and out, moaning with the joy of it, coating it with saliva. Then, quickly, she moved it down to her lower lips.

Pressing the head with her other hand, she ran it along the warm, slippery furrow of her pussy lips, up and down a few times until it lodged at the entrance to her sex. Pushing it in, she could feel the final build up to orgasm starting.

"I'm gonna come." Cassie declared. "Gonna come real soon." She started pushing the dildo in and out of herself, faster and harder as she became more and more excited. "Come for me!" she called out. "Let me see you come!"

Noel's hand was pumping up and down his shaft fast now. He had dropped forward and supported himself on his free hand, so that his cock was right over the tablet where it lay on his bed. Cassie could see the head bobbing around as the fist around it moved faster, and she could hear his breathing speeding up.

With a cry, Noel came. Cassie watched big white blobs splattering down onto the screen of her laptop as they landed around the camera of a tablet all the way away in England. She came hard, the orgasm shaking through her body and coming out as a series of panted cries. She kept moving the dildo in herself, teasing out a second and third climax while Noel hunched over the tablet on the other side of the world.

They made happy post-coital sounds for long minutes after they had finished, then the image on Cassie's laptop changed. She had just become used to staring at a grey and white pattern where semen lay over the tablet's lens, when Noel began wiping it away. He reappeared through the smears, smiling dreamily. "It seems to be come proof, but I'm still not sure about waterproof." he said. Then he looked at the screen for a while, quietly enjoying the view.

Cassie had the dildo in her right hand, resting on her thigh. It curved gently over, the head teasingly close to her sex. Her left hand had been gently stroking a breast and teasing at the nipple, but when she realised Noel could see her again, she reached down with it and released the two buttons that fastened the skirt together. She pulled the skirt away from herself and dropped it to the floor. As if realising that she still held the dildo, she brought it lazily up to her mouth and kissed the head. She ran her tongue around it, tasting her own juices and loving the flavour, then took it between her lips and sucked a length of it in. Noel made a horny sighing sound as he watched.

Putting the dildo aside, Cassie grinned at her lover. Then she reached down between her legs and found the base of the butt plug. Angling her hips, she made sure the camera had a good view. She could see Noel's anticipation in the way he bit his lower lip as she clasped the base and started pulling the toy, slowly, out. As much as her body had resisted its entry at first, now it held tight, reluctant to let it go. The tight ring of muscle gripped it, but eased slowly wider as the flared section pushed through it. A shiver of pleasure, not quite another orgasm, ran through Cassie when the plug eventually popped out. She dropped it onto paper towels she had arranged on the floor to help with cleaning up, and made a sighing, moaning sound.

"You've got me all turned on again now." Noel said.

"Well, I'm going to tease you for a while, then. There are still some more toys in the box. Maybe I'll get them out later, if you're good, or maybe I'll save them for next week."

Cassie On Top

Cassie's toes could just reach the floor. She was lifted up in a kiss she had waited four weeks for. She had wrapped her arms around Noel as soon as she had found him, pulling his lips to hers. As the kiss had stretched out, he had reached down to cup her buttocks and lift her as he straightened. It didn't matter that the business of the airport arrivals hall swirled around them, they were lost in their embrace.

When she had to come up for air, Cassie moved her lips to Noel's ear and whispered, "Did you get my message?"

"The shag wagon awaits." he replied, just as quietly. Cassie couldn't help but laugh.

Noel let Cassie down onto her feet again and, when she had regained her balance, she cradled his head in her hands and brought it down to kiss him with quick pecks all over. Then she mouthed, "I'm so horny right now."

"Well, let's get your suitcase first, then get to the van." Noel said, offering his hand to lead her to baggage retrieval.

* * *

"THIS ISN'T THE SUITCASE you took with you." Noel commented, looking down at the bag he was pulling across the concrete of the car park.

"It's Megumi-san's. I needed a bigger case, for all the new clothes and toys I bought while I was there, so I swapped with her. She'll bring it when she comes here, and we'll swap back then."

"She's coming to Britain? I'd quite like to meet the lovely Megumi." Cassie had told Noel lots of naughty things about her co-worker and neighbour in Japan.

"I'm sure you would, you dirty man." They had reached the van, a blue short wheelbase Transit showing the dents and rust of the active life it had

37

enjoyed before Noel had bought it. He was going to use it to carry loads of not-quite-antiques from the auctions where he and his business partner bought them to the unit where they repaired and re-purposed the furniture before selling it on. But today it would serve a different purpose.

Noel had parked in a corner of the car park, with the passenger side of the van facing the concrete wall. When they walked round to the sliding side door, they were almost completely hidden from view. Noel dragged the door open and lifted the suitcase into the van. Cassie stepped forward and put her backpack beside the case, then studied the interior.

The load space of the van was even more battered than the exterior, but, taking up a fair amount of the floor space, was a camping air bed, inflated and ready to use. Which was just what Cassie had requested. She felt Noel close behind her, and sensed the warmth of his body and his excitement, which matched hers. "The shag wagon is ready, isn't it." she said.

Noel's left arm wrapped around Cassie's chest, pulling her close to him so that he could whisper, "Are you ready?" His right hand had moved down to the front of her light trousers and started squeezing the big top button through its eye.

Cassie held her breath. They were in a public place, she remembered, someone could come along.

She didn't care, she realised as the button popped open. She silently willed Noel on to release the remaining two buttons that held the trousers up. Noel nibbled her earlobe as he tugged at the next button. Cassie was glad he had a hold on her, because her legs were beginning to tremble and she wasn't sure how long she could stay stood up.

The last button on the trousers opened. Noel stroked his fingers across the cotton of Cassie's knickers, and she was sure he could feel how damp she was through the material. With a shimmy of her hips, she shook the trousers loose. Splaying her knees, she caught them before they slid all the way to her ankles.

Cassie wasn't naked, but her underwear was on display, and it would be obvious to anyone who saw them what they were up to. The thought turned her on more than she could ever have imagined. When Noel's fingers moved down again and tugged the knickers aside, he found her lips puffed up and slippery. Two fingers slid into her incredibly easily, all the way up to the second knuckle.

Noel's thumb rested on the sheath over Cassie's clitoris, rubbing the sensitive bud beneath as his fingers moved in circles inside her. She twisted her head so that they could kiss clumsily.

Somewhere in the car park, tyres squealed on concrete as a car turned a corner. Noel's fingers stopped moving, and they both held their breath. The tyres squealed again, quieter, as the car turned another corner, further away. They nearly fell over as they laughed so hard it was hard to breathe.

Cassie pulled her trousers up to the top of her thighs, and Noel let go of her so that she could climb into the van. He followed her, and pulled the door closed.

Stretched out on the air bed, Cassie already had her trousers and knickers down to her calves. Having trouble getting them off completely, she raised her feet in the air and waggled them. Getting the message, Noel quickly moved to pull them off, dropping them onto her suitcase.

Crouched between Cassie's long legs, Noel's gaze ran up them to her crotch. He stared at the pink folds of her open sex, uneven tear drop shapes one inside the other, demanding his attention. She reached up to him. "I need you in me now." He needed no more encouragement.

Noel flipped a wrapped condom out of his pocket, and Cassie ripped the foil off as he pushed his trousers and boxers down to his knees. She handed the sheath back to him and he rolled it down his stiff shaft. He leant forward, planting his hands either side of her and bending to kiss her.

All the weeks they had been apart, Cassie had been waiting to do this again. She was wet with anticipation, and her sex opened up to Noel and invited him in. He found her without needing any guidance or a helping hand, and they both let out a little gasp as her warmth enclosed the head of his erection.

Noel slid easily but slowly into Cassie, until he lay on top of her as they kissed. Her arms and legs wrapped around him and held him in place. "I just need to feel you in me." she said, between kisses. "That's so good."

They lay together, savouring the contact they had missed whilst Cassie was away, listening to the sounds of the car park and the airport beyond. There was the squeal of another car's wheels on the concrete paving, but this one was right behind the van, and it made them both jump.

The car had simply been turning the corner behind the van, and they could hear it driving away. Cassie giggled, but she couldn't deny the fact that knowing people could pass so close by whilst they made love in the van was an incredible turn on. "Fuck me." she said.

Noel pulled slowly out of Cassie. She was hot and wet, but it still felt as if the sheath around his cock was holding as tight as it could, trying to grip him and keep him in place. It was exquisite. Cassie's long legs relaxed enough to let him move in and out of her with slow, short thrusts.

They tried to keep their lovemaking as quiet and gentle as they could, but Cassie was soon urging Noel on to faster, harder and longer thrusts. He lifted himself up, straightening his arms to hold himself above her as he pushed into her. She reached down and lifted the hem of her top, biting down on it to keep from squealing at the mounting pleasure she felt.

Cassie was close- so very close- to coming. She could feel it building, inside her at the deepest point that Noel reached at the end of each thrust. The climax was going to come pulsing out of her soon, radiating through her body. Her arms wrapped around Noel's, and her hips bucked in time with his thrusts. The material of her top slipped out of her mouth, and her cries filled the inside of the van as her orgasm rippled through her.

Noel's thrusts slowed as he dipped his head down to kiss Cassie. Their tongues played together as her climax drew out, hitting a succession of little peaks as he kept on moving inside her. With a grunt muffled between their lips, he made one last thrust and Cassie could feel the pulses in his penis as he, too, came.

* * *

THEY LAY TOGETHER FOR a while, cuddling, savouring the skin to skin contact they had been deprived of. Then there were more tyre squeals nearby, and Cassie said, "We should leave, before security gets suspicious."

"Or I have to sell the van to be able to afford the cost of the parking." Noel pulled the filled condom off his still half hard cock and tied it. He found a box of paper handkerchiefs he had stored for just this occasion, and wrapped the condom in a couple. He pulled his trousers up and handed Cassie hers.

"Where are my knickers?"

"I thought I'd keep those." Noel said, grinning.

Cassie thought about protesting, but decided she really liked the idea of going commando. The trousers were lightweight, she could almost pretend they weren't there at all. She still squeaked with shock when Noel opened the side door. "Just going to pay at the machine." he said. She gave him an exaggerated scowl as he stepped from the van.

The vehicle smelt of sex, Cassie thought when she had moved to the front passenger seat. She smelt of sex, she told herself with a grin. Spreading her legs, she imagined she could sense the sharp musk of her sex. Through the thin material of her trousers, the air felt cold against the warmth of her crotch. She released the second and third buttons on the front of the trousers and opened the gap with a pair of fingers to let more of the cool air in. Looking around, she could see Noel approaching in the driver side door mirror, so she wasn't surprised when his door opened.

Noel looked across at Cassie, who had closed her eyes and was smiling at her naughtiness. "I love you, you dirty, naughty girl." he said, and leant across to kiss her cheek.

"I'm just going to get dirtier and naughtier." Cassie said.

"Good, just what I wanted to hear. Now belt up, and I'll take you home."

"For more sex?"

"If you don't fall asleep on me."

"I'm not going to do that. I heard about a way to beat jet lag by staying up until you'd normally go to bed then sleeping through and getting up at a normal time. It's supposed to reset your body clock. So I need you to keep me awake until, I don't know, nine o'clock at least."

"What am I going to do to keep you awake for the next twelve and a bit hours?"

"I'm sure we can think of something."

＊ ＊ ＊

AFTER NEARLY A MONTH apart, Cassie wanted to be naked with her lover, and the best place to start was in the shower. Sweaty and a bit sticky after making love in the van, they both needed a steamy clean anyway. They parked Cassie's bags in the hallway outside the bathroom, and she started discarding clothes before Noel had even finished locking the door. With her bra and top in one hand, and the trousers down around her ankles, she waved her free finger at him, signalling that he needed to follow her example. He wasn't going to argue.

There was just enough room in the shower for both of them, so Cassie had to press right up against Noel's chest. He wasn't complaining. She did a little shimmy and rotated her nipples around his until they both giggled. Reaching down, she squeezed his balls, then rubbed soapy water up and down his stiffening shaft. "I have missed this so much. Y'know what I wanna do with it?"

"What do you want to do with it?"

"Everything. You know where I want you to put it?"

"Everywhere?" Noel said, with a big grin.

"Everywhere." Cassie whispered. "Every. Where. Now, rinse off and go and wait for me on the bed so I can get ready for you."

Noel stretched out on the bed, hands crossed behind his head and a faraway grin on his lips. He didn't know what Cassie was preparing, but it took her a long time to do it. When she walked, naked, into the bedroom, his penis was fat and heavy and more than ready to rise quickly as soon as Cassie came in.

Cassie entered the room quietly, almost demurely, holding something behind her back, keeping it hidden from him. Noel had expected her to be naked, but she had actually got dressed up. She was wearing an outfit she had bought whilst in Japan, a naughty cosplay school uniform. The navy blue pleated skirt was so short that she was in danger of flashing her naked crotch as she moved. She wore no bra under the tightly cut blouse, and the white wing collars were opened to reveal cleavage. She may not have been wearing any underwear, but she had put on the flat pumps and white leg warmers which bunched up just below her knees.

"Remember this?" Cassie said, grinning and flushing a little.

"Do I ever." Cassie had worn the outfit for most of a very dirty video chat they had had while she was in Japan. The memories made Noel's erection strain up, harder and stiffer.

"And this?" Cassie's left hand came out from behind her back, to show him the purple butt plug she had used during their chat. Noel remembered her turning around and showing him as she pushed it slowly into her. He nodded. He hadn't thought he could get any harder. "Well, I got a slightly bigger one, and I want you to put it up my arse." Cassie revealed the contents of her right hand. The toy she held out was pale blue, soft enough to bend a little as she held it by the base, and modelled after a penis. It wasn't as thick, or as long, as Noel's hard on- which was beginning to throb almost painfully with desire- but realistic in its scaled down way. Pressed up against it was a tube of lubricant.

Cassie climbed onto the end of the bed, then leant forward so that her mouth hovered over Noel's penis. He could feel her breath on it as she said, "And later, when I'm ready, I want you to replace it with this." She kissed the base of the hard on. "I told you I wanted it everywhere." She gently held a testicle between her lips and teased it with the tip of her tongue.

"Come here, dirty manga girl. I need to kiss you." Noel managed to say.

Cassie slinked up the bed, moving slowly and deliberately, watching Noel's expression as she drew closer. She didn't mind in the slightest that his gaze dropped and he stared down the open collar of her top to watch her breasts as they swayed gently. The hem of her short skirt hung down and trailed up the skin of his thighs, then his balls and erection, which made him shiver. Just before she made the final move to kiss him, she made sure the material pulled the last little bit to drop off the head of Noel's cock. As she lay down on him, his hard on was between the pleated material and the skin of her crotch. The thick hair of her pubes teased at the head, and warm, wet lips parted as they rested on the base of the shaft.

"You're a dirty girl, and I love you." Noel said.

Punctuating with kisses, Cassie said, "You bring out the best in me. Or the worst. The dirtiest. Definitely the dirtiest."

Feeling the length of her lover where he pressed against her, Cassie thought of how she wanted it in her. Then, how she was going to try to get it up her back passage. She had tried anal play before, and been incredibly turned on doing it for Noel on video, but she was no rear entry expert. She was nervous, and incredibly turned on, at the thought of it. Holding up the larger butt plug, she said, "Let's get this inside me!"

The task proved more complicated, and comical, than expected, as Cassie shuffled around into a sort of 69, but with her crotch resting on Noel's chest, rather than hovering over his face. Her mouth was back at the base of his lovely cock, so she could kiss his balls and tease him as he went about his work.

Finally ready, Cassie relaxed. Then she tensed up again as Noel flipped the back of her short skirt up and revealed her private parts. Despite everything they had done together, no matter that she had shown him the wrinkled hole of her behind several times before, and that she had already fingered some lube up it so that the entrance glistened with it and was ready for him, she still felt a twinge of shame that he could see so private a part of her. She was finding, however, that nowadays that the sense of shame quickly gave way to an erotic charge. The more she imagined people being shocked at such behaviour, or the stronger the feeling that someone could see her doing such disgusting things, the hotter it made her feel.

Noel could surely feel the heat from her groin, Cassie thought. She was so hot, and so wet, just from thinking about what they were about to do. She felt one of his hands stroking up her thighs and then around the taut curves of her buttocks. His fingers separated her cheeks even more than they were already splayed, and she felt her sphincter open a little to his view, almost pouting at him. Such disgusting behaviour from a good girl, so, so very erotic.

With the butt plug in one hand and the tube of lube in the other, Noel squeezed a glistening drop of lubricant onto the head. Then he presented it to Cassie's hole. The long, thin plug wasn't rigid, and bent as he pushed it from the base, hardly pressing into Cassie at all. It would work perfectly well once it was in her, but right now, it needed some more persuasion.

Cassie relaxed, as much as she could, and Noel moved his grip down the shaft. He pushed, and she moved her body back to meet it, and the head of the plug eased in cleanly. Cassie bit her bottom lip as Noel began pressing the long toy into her, letting go to sigh as she practically sucked the rest of it into her all the way to the flared base.

They lay together for a while, Noel marvelling at the view, Cassie waiting for her heart rate to drop a bit. Her breathing was heavy, she realised as she watched Noel's pubic hair dancing in the breeze. She moved closer to his shaft, to kiss it, and watched, amused, as his balls pulled up into his body, the wrinkled skin of his scrotum tightening as it followed them.

Noel started massaging Cassie's buttocks, squeezing them together and pulling them apart so that the plug moved inside her. She liked that. She liked it even more when he urged her backwards so that she was hovering over his face. His tongue sneaked out to lick along her slit and taste her excitement.

Two buttons held Cassie's skirt up. She reached back and released them, then pulled it off and threw it aside. Noel's tongue had split her lips and was inside her, and she rotated her hips to move it around. She moved backwards, and Noel started flicking the tip of his tongue around her clitoris. Grasping the sheets and holding her position against the intensity of it, Cassie's moan rose in volume and pitch. When Noel hooked fingers around the base of the butt plug and started moving it in and out, it was all too much for Cassie, and she had to lift away from his tongue.

Noel's cock was solid and hot and twitching up toward Cassie's mouth. All the attention he'd given her, and she had yet to do anything more than just tease him. She bent forward and took the head between her lips. It tasted of pre-cum, and felt hot and slick. She took the whole of the head into her mouth and pressed her tongue against it, moving with the thrusts of the plug in her butt.

It was too much. Cassie needed the hard penis where the slick plug was, and she needed it right away. She let Noel's cock slip from her lips and said, almost as a grunt, "I want you in me now."

Cassie swung her leg over and slid off the bed. As Noel reached out for the drawer he kept the condoms in- trying not to take his eyes off her- Cassie found it hard to stand steady. She watched as he rolled the sheath down his length and squirted lube onto it. Fumbling, she undid her top and shrugged out of it. Still wearing the socks and pumps, she was now naked from the knees up.

Noel held out his hand, and Cassie took it and let him help her onto the bed. She straddled him, hovering above him, suddenly nervous. Even before the first time she had had sex, she hadn't been this nervous, she was sure. It was excitement as well, she wasn't sure how this was going to go. Noel held his erection up, pointing it toward the target. Cassie started lowering herself toward it. She felt the tip touch her right buttock and then slip between them. Noel moved it a little and it slid between them until it found the mark.

Cassie reminded herself she had just had a toy up there. She could take this too. She sank down a little, and it pushed at her ring, but it wouldn't go in. Why couldn't she open up to Noel's cock?

Seeing the confusion, which could easily slip toward panic, Noel reached up to take Cassie's forearms. Distracted by the touch, she looked down at him.

His expression was equal parts love and lust. He lightly squeezed her arms and quietly said, "It's okay, don't try to force it. Go gently."

Cassie stared down at Noel, reading the reassurance in his smile. She decided to concentrate on his handsome face for a while, and not think about anything else. He had blue eyes, deeper blue than hers, that she could get lost in, and a square jaw and awesome cheekbones. Something was pressing at her rear, and she decided to just let it in.

Eyes wide, Cassie realised that the head of Noel's cock had just pushed past the ring of muscle of her sphincter. He was inside her, and he'd made it in without any fuss once she'd relaxed. Now that she was aware of it again, she could feel the strain of her butt hole as it was pushed out to accommodate him. It was intense, it hurt, but it also gave her a great erotic thrill. She had never let anyone do this to her before, this was a level of intimacy greater than she had ever shared with another.

Noel's lips were parted, but he couldn't seem to form any words. He laced his fingers between hers, and she balanced against them as she eased herself down and let his length feed into her. "That's tight." he said, quietly.

Cassie couldn't reply, she was squatting down further, letting him fill her up. He was deep inside her, going deeper and deeper. She knew she could take it now, and was determined to have the whole of him inside her. Letting out a low moan, she nestled down on Noel's cock, all the way, until she was resting in his lap.

"This is incredible." Cassie said as she moved her hands to rest them on Noel's chest. She lifted her butt up, leaning forward, sighing as she felt the head of Noel's cock moving in her and she bent to kiss him. "I'm going to need you to move in me." she said when she had rocked back and forth a few more times.

Noel kissed Cassie's cheeks and reached down to clasp her butt cheeks and pull them apart. Rocking his hips, he began moving inside her, sending tingles and a sharp sensation that was an exquisite mix of pleasure and pain through her body. She buried her head in his shoulder and closed her eyes to soak up the sensations.

Cassie hadn't known what to expect once Noel was inside her, whether she would come or not. As he moved inside her, she could feel something building in her. Not a normal orgasm, it came from a different part of her, but it was going to be intense, and it was going to break over her any moment. Her fingers dug into Noel's shoulders as she readied herself for it.

A pulse of release passed through Cassie's body. She couldn't help but twitch and shake, making little squeaks and squeals as it moved through her to its own beat. Her passage tightened up as she tensed the muscles, and Noel felt even bigger inside her as she squeezed him. His gasps joined Cassie's noises of pleasure.

One of Noel's hands was stroking Cassie's hair, gently urging her to lift her head and bring her lips to his. She kissed her way up his cheek, then their mouths and tongues met to play against each other. Remembering his gasp, Cassie lifted herself to look down at Noel. "I didn't hurt you, did I?"

"No. Oh hell no, that was incredible. Squeeze me again."

Cassie watched Noel's far away expression as she clenched her buttocks. He definitely liked that, she needn't have worried about hurting him. She released the tension, then squeezed him again. If she could keep it up, she would be able to milk Noel's cock just by doing this. He started moving in her again, to give a bit of help.

The piston of Noel's cock in Cassie's arse started to move faster as he drew closer to coming himself. She held still, squeezing him when her self control allowed it, and revelled in the expression on his face as he filled the condom deep inside her.

* * *

CASSIE WAS WARM AND happy. She ached a little, but it was a good, warm feeling. Just like the sensations after exercising. Which was what they had done, in a way, Noel had stretched the muscles of her back passage. She clenched. Were they stronger? Could she exercise them like she did with her pelvic floor? She'd have to find out.

Noel's arms were wrapped around her, one hand clasping a breast, and his soft, but still long and fat, dick was pressed between their bodies. "I fell asleep, didn't I?"

"You did."

"So much for my jet lag busting plan."

"You were only asleep for a little while. We can still try keeping you awake for a few more hours."

"And how will we do that?"

"More of the same?"

"I don't know if I'm ready to do that again. It was incredible. I came. I didn't know whether I'd come, but.... It was incredible. I've already said that haven't I? I'm babbling. Anyway, I definitely want to do that again, but not today. Okay?"

"Okay."

Half an hour later, after another shower, Cassie was stretched out on the bed again, on her front on a large blanket. Noel straddled her legs, rubbing his hands together to warm the oil on them. A massage might relax Cassie and send her to sleep again, but she would risk it. She wanted to feel his hands all over her.

Noel went straight for the obvious targets, hands cupping her butt cheeks and kneading them. Cassie didn't mind at all, she was loving the attention her backside was receiving today. The circling of Noel's hands pulled her buttocks apart then squeezed them together, teasing her recently exercised hole and warming her all the way through. She would definitely let him fuck her there again, she thought, but it was still a little too tender to do it again today.

The warming, soothing hands moved down to Cassie's thighs. Concentrating on the right thigh first, Noel twisted his hands against each other, then squeezed and kneaded any tension from them. A gentle hand behind her knee moved her leg out, and Noel lifted his so that it was inside hers. She smiled, she knew what he was doing, and she liked it.

Repeating the kneading and spreading on Cassie's left leg, Noel was soon crouched between her thighs and she was open to him. She resisted the temptation to flex her hips and show him more of her already warm and wet pussy. His hands came up to her waist, then went away briefly as he put more massage oil on them.

Noel ran his hands up Cassie's back, thumbs either side of her spine, until they reached her shoulders. Leaning forward like this, the warm length of his erection rested between Cassie's buttocks. This time she couldn't control her body, and pushed up gently, to squeeze the lovely cock between their bodies again. It rubbed against her tender and sensitive arse hole and sent happy and dirty memories through her body.

Cassie made happy sounds as Noel squeezed and worked on the muscles in her shoulders. All the while, she was drawing her knees up and lifting her backside higher, pushing against him and making it easier for him to slip into her when he moved back down. He had noticed this and said, quietly, "You want some massaging from the inside, eh?" She wiggled her butt against him as a response.

Noel sat back for a moment. Cassie took the opportunity to lift her butt higher. With her head still on the bed and her privates up in the air, it was obvious Cassie was ready for sex. But, just in case Noel hadn't got the message, she reached back with one hand and split the wet lips of her pussy with her fingers. Condom on, Noel presented the head of his cock to the entrance. Holding her about the waist, he pushed into her.

Oh yes, Cassie told herself, if we can keep this up, I'll be more than able to stay awake long enough to put the jet lag to bed.

Cassie On Show

The text read, 'Dr says implants effective by Sunday. I'm time for me getting back. ;-)' Noel couldn't keep the grin down. He stroked the screen gently, like it was the body of the lover who had sent the text, as he closed the message.

"You just got a booty call, didn't you? You're going to leave us here." said Tony. "And after I just bought you a pint."

"I shall not desert you tonight." Noel intoned with mock seriousness. "The booty is at home with her parents. She'll be back after the weekend."

"You lucky, lucky man."

"Says the guy who just got engaged. Tonight we celebrate...." Noel turned to Emma, who sat on the other side of him. "Do we celebrate or commiserate? I'm not sure."

"He's marrying my best friend, so we celebrate. If she was marrying you, maybe we'd commiserate with her."

"You're horrible. Where is the bride to be?"

"She went home to show her parents the ring." Tony said.

"And convince her father to put the shotgun away?"

"She's not pregnant. Why does everyone think she's pregnant?"

"Because it winds you up so much."

"And you say Emma's horrible."

Noel raised his pint glass and tipped it toward Tony. "Congratulations, dude."

They clinked glasses, and Emma reached across to join in the tinkling.

"Where's Steve?" Emma asked after finishing her drink.

"Where's everyone?" said Tony. "I'm not so miserable that you're my only friends."

"Steve's been painting furniture all afternoon. He's probably gone home to wash the paint off. I've had a few texts saying people are running late. They'll be here eventually." Noel studied his nearly empty glass, then emptied it in one go. Taking Emma's glass and pointing at Tony's half full pint, he said, "Same again?"

Standing at the bar as the pints were pulled, Noel replied to the text. '<3 Looking forward to it. Bagsy on top! ;-P'

He'd started thinking about sex with Cassie now. Something about the heightened intimacy made him want the first time they made love without a sheath to be something simple like the missionary position. They could be face to face and skin to skin, really revelling in it. As the bar man planted the pints on the bar, with napkins under them catching the dribble of excess head down the sides, Noel realised he had a hard on that was going to tent out his light trousers and be far too obvious as he carried the drinks back to the table.

* * *

HUNGOVER, NOEL STARED over the side of the bed at the screen of his phone. He had dug it out of his trouser pocket some time earlier to stop the alarm, then dropped it back to the floor. He vaguely remembered it beeping at him some time in the last hour and a bit, during one of the periods when he'd been more or less awake.

Reaching out carefully, he poked the phone until the screen lit up, then clumsily went through the sequence of swipes and presses needed to get at his messages. Cassie had sent him a picture. The note that accompanied it said, 'Something to wake you up after all the beer you had last night.' He pressed the icon for the image.

The picture helped Noel wake up in the best possible way. It took him a moment to realise it was upside down, not that that mattered. Cassie had stretched out somewhere, spread her thighs and put her phone between them to take a picture.

Noel loved the lips he was looking at now. They were pouting open just a little, emphasising the tear drop shape of the entrance to Cassie's vagina. He could see inside her a short way, and noticed the way the bud of her clitoris was peeking out ever so slightly. But the really interesting part of the image was what wasn't there. The top third of the image showed bare skin where previously there had been hair. There was a slight hint of redness, where Cassie had shaved herself, but the patch where her pubes had been was now only marked by slightly paler skin.

Already hard, Noel knew what he had to do. He threw aside the sheets and picked up his phone. As a keen photographer, though, he had to take some time to find the right angle and compose the picture. So he ended up with half a dozen photos of his erect penis to choose from. 'A reply in kind coming your way soon. :-) Don't open in front of family.' he sent whilst working out which image to use.

Nearly an hour later, when he had managed to get out of bed, shower and shave and was just settling down to a breakfast so late that it was lunch, Noel received a reply to his dick pic. 'Mum's taken me bra shopping :-S. But I got a chance to take this.' the message read. The attached picture was a close up of Cassie's left nipple, pink, stiff and pointing out at the thought of being photographed.

Noel stroked the curve of Cassie's nipple on the screen. He would remember to show it extra attention when she got back. Another message arrived. 'Got some other pics for you to enjoy. Not of me, though....' That was intriguing. Noel had an inclination who they would be of, and was eager to find out what they involved. Almost as eager as he was to make love to his girlfriend again. Either way, he had to wait until the next afternoon, so he had to find something to keep himself busy in the mean time.

* * *

"WHAT ARE ALL THE PICTURE frames for?" Cassie asked, distracted by the pile of mounting board on the table in the corner of the room.

"I made them up yesterday for all the prints I'm getting of my photos." Noel was stood behind her, waiting to reach down and lift her skirt.

"Oh yeah. I remember you mentioned them."

"It was a nice simple job to do whilst hungover and horny."

Cassie giggled and turned her head to look back over her shoulder in a way that could have been coy. "You liked the pictures I sent, then?"

"Loved them. Almost as much as the real thing."

"If you want the real thing, you should lift my skirt up."

Noel did as he was told. It wasn't the shortest of Cassie's skirts, almost reaching her knees and overlapping her black thigh high stockings. Lifting the hem, Noel ran his finger up the stockings, then over the skin of her thighs. He stopped when he was sure he should have encountered the edge of her underwear, but hadn't.

Cassie was holding back a laugh as Noel held up her skirt and searched around to confirm she was wearing nothing under it. When he was sure of it, he reached around to run is hand over the hairless spot where her pubic hair had been just days before. "You naughty girl." he whispered, "Have you had no knickers on all the way here."

"Not all the way. I took them off in the toilets about an hour ago. I loved the feeling of knowing I could accidentally flash someone if I wasn't careful. It really turned me on." To illustrate, Cassie laid a hand on top of Noel's and guided it down to her lips. They were warm and, when Noel pressed a finger between them, slick with her excitement. He kissed her neck as he pushed a second finger into her and started rotating them in her.

Reaching back, Cassie tugged Noel's head around until she could get him in a kiss. Just the sides of their mouths touched, but their tongues played against each other. Her other hand sneaked between their bodies and found the front of his trousers. Noel broke their kiss to say, "Bedroom?"

"Here." Cassie said. Pointing at the window, she added, "Over there."

Noel let her lead him over to the window. Planting her feet apart, Cassie leant forward and placed her hands on the sill. "I couldn't get this image out of my head all the way here." she said. "Let's do it here, where people might see us."

Noel's flat was on the corner of his building, and the windows of the kitchen and living room faced in a different direction to those of the bedroom. There were no buildings overlooking the bedroom, so they had often made love and wandered around naked with the curtains open. On this side of the building, however, there were neighbours across the road who could, if they were inclined, look in through Noel's windows.

The possibility of being seen turned Cassie on. Her exhibitionism, it seemed, was something she had only begun to discover with the start of their relationship. It had first come out when they filmed themselves making love, just before she had headed to Japan. The idea of having an audience had excited her, and anything that got Cassie hot was a thing that Noel approved of. Plus, he was finding that he enjoyed it as well.

Stepping closer, Noel turned up Cassie's skirt to reveal her buttocks. They were lovely. Shapely but just soft enough to knead and play with. He parted them, revealing the puckered ring of her arse, which twitched as if reacting to his gaze. That wasn't where he was going just yet, though. Going down on his knees he shuffled a little closer.

"What are you...?" Cassie started to ask, the end of her question cut off into a long sigh as Noel pressed his tongue first to the newly naked skin above her mons and then the lips below it. He pushed deep into her, tasting her excitement and getting her even more wet.

Cassie was ready. She had been ready before Noel had gone down on her, but the attention of his tongue was always welcome. He stood, unzipping his trousers and dropping them and his underwear. As he pressed his hips forwards, the tip of his erection ran over the wet lips of Cassie's sex. He pulled back, retracing its route, then reached down to guide his aim when he pushed forwards again.

Noel was sure that he could feel every wrinkle inside Cassie, particularly when he hit the bump of her G spot on the front wall and she let out a little purr. Some of it might have been imagined, but there was no denying that being inside his lover without a condom on was an incredible sensation. He felt his skin touching hers, the warmth, the slick sensations of their juices. It was another level of intimacy, bringing them even closer than before. He grasped her hips and started to build his rhythm moving in and out of her.

Cassie's breath was misting on the window pane as she started panting and moaning. She had been fantasising all the way here, and was already incredibly turned on. "Harder." she said, the order coming out mumbled and mixed with a grunt as Noel reached the end of a thrust. He complied, pulling her toward him when he began his next thrust, pushing, it felt, even deeper into her.

They had both worked themselves up to excitement just thinking about being together, and it wasn't long before Noel's legs began to quiver and his thrusts became less controlled. Cassie pushed back against him, but she was close as well, tremors building in her thighs and the bare skin she had shaved the day before flushing and glowing.

Noel came first, just, clasping her close to him as he pumped semen deep inside her, properly flooding her insides for the first time. She ground against him, pushing herself over the edge. Her muscles clasped his erection, holding it inside her and trying to milk it of every last drop. Head pressed against the window, she pushed back against Noel, rotating her hips and crying out happily as after shocks passed through her.

They stayed like that for a while, aware of the sounds of traffic and bird life from outside the window. Grinning, Cassie scanned the windows across the road. There was no obvious sign of anyone staring back, which was almost a disappointment.

Noel pulled out, and his juices started dribbling from Cassie. She stayed as she was- legs spread and hands resting on the window sill- and felt herself dripping onto the floor. It was another incredibly dirty, and therefore intoxicating, sensation. Noel leaned forward to kiss her. They stayed like that for a while longer, Cassie shivering with taboo pleasure every time a little bit of Noel's come slipped from her to stain the floor.

* * *

"THE WET SPOT COULD be a problem." Cassie admitted later. She was sitting cross-legged on the couch in the living room, wearing only a T-shirt that wasn't quite long enough to be modest.

"I can live with a few stains." Noel said.

"Yeah, but, in bed? I don't want to roll into it in the middle of the night."

"We'll just have to do it everywhere but the bed."

"That's tempting. But let's keep, I don't know, a towel or something in the bedroom to soak it up."

"Okay." Noel was distracted. He'd just looked down and noticed how high the hem of Cassie's T-shirt was. He was reaching down to move it higher. He caught a glimpse of Cassie's expression, and grinned. "Sorry. You're shaved pussy fascinates me."

"That was the plan." Cassie untangled her legs and stretched them out. Lifting the hem, she let Noel look and touch. His finger ran around the now naked skin where she had shaved off her pubic hair, and it was a lot more sensitive than she had expected. "Give me a kiss." she demanded, and he did.

Noel's fingers moved lower, and worked their way into Cassie as they kissed. With little twists and thrusts, they soon had her working toward orgasm. Noel slid off the couch and moved between Cassie's legs, kissing and licking her newly bald mound as his fingers continued their work. When his tongue began lapping at the hood of her clitoris, she came quickly, grasping his hair to hold him in place a little longer.

When Cassie let him go, Noel sat back. He teased her as he pulled his fingers from her, then took them into his mouth and sucked the taste of her from them. Cassie shivered, it always turned her on to see him do that.

"We were talking about something." Cassie said, dreamily, after a while.

"Wet spots, I think."

"Oh, right." Cassie's eyebrows raised as she remembered something. Bouncing, she sat up quickly and pointed at the bag she had left by the door. "Bring me my laptop, there's some stuff for me to show you." She watched the movements of the bulge in the front of his boxers as he walked across the room and licked her lips.

Noel brought the bag over and let Cassie delve in it herself to find her laptop. She pulled it out and put it on her lap, then had a thought and handed it to Noel. "Can you plug it into the TV?"

When the laptop was hooked up, the cable didn't reach all the way to the couch, so Cassie sat halfway between them. Noel was on the couch behind her, enjoying the sneaky flashes he got of her buttocks as she worked her way through folders. "There we are." she said, and he finally looked up at the television screen.

On the screen was a picture of a pretty Japanese girl standing before a futon in a small room. The walls were covered with posters of animé and video game characters. Her costume, a sexualised pastiche of a French maid's outfit, could have come from one of the posters. It was a confection in deep blacks and crisp white. The skirt flared out dramatically below the waist, buoyed on clouds of puffy lace, exposing shapely legs. The girl's white-gloved hands were clasped together and pressing down at the end of straight arms, so that she was leaning forward and pushing her butt out. Her grin could only be described as cheeky, knowing that she looked both incredibly sexy and simultaneously a bit silly.

"That's Megumi?" Noel asked as another picture came up, showing her in a different silly pose.

"Isn't she gorgeous?" When Noel didn't answer, Cassie craned her head back to stare up at him and smile. "It's okay, you can admit it. I thinks she's beautiful." Quietly, as if sharing a secret, she added, "I've got a bit of a crush on her."

The picture changed again. Megumi was still in the maid outfit. Now, she had turned to face the camera. Her left leg was kicked out and the foot twisted so the toes still touched the ground. Her left forefinger was up to her pursed lips, false expression of surprise on her face, whilst her right had reached down to lift and bunch all the under skirts and expose her white thong.

Cassie shuffled backwards some more, until the back of her head butted up against Noel's erection where it pushed out the material of his boxers. She teased him for a while, moving her head from side to side to rub him, then reached back to squeeze him as the picture changed again. Megumi was in a different outfit, a titillating spin on the Disney cartoon Alice, in a too short blue and white dress and a long blonde wig.

"You do like her." Cassie said as she stroked Noel through the cotton. "He likes her, anyway. Let him out for me."

"He's in a room with a hot woman, he was already happy." Noel said, but his protest was undermined by the speed with which he reached down to unbutton his boxers and let the erection out. As Megumi worked her way through some more sexy cute poses, Cassie closed two fingers on Noel's shaft and moved them up and down, teasing him.

The costume changed again, and this one was in a completely different style. Gone were the near puffball skirts and lace detailing, replaced by shiny dark blue hot pants with a wide white belt, a bikini top and cape in the same colour and calf length white vinyl boots. She was holding the cape open, with a toy gun in one hand and a sheathed katana in the other. Her hair arced out from the top of her head in two pigtails, curving down to join under her chin. Noel was certain he recognised the outfit from a video game he'd played, years before.

"This is where she said she'd get seriously naughty." Cassie said, shuffling around so that she could clasp Noel with all her fingers.

He would have been turned on anyway, sitting on the couch with his girlfriend giving him a hand job, but the pictures were taking it to another level. Megumi had sent them halfway around the world, part of her payback for getting to watch a video of Cassie and Noel making love. He was looking forward to meeting the gorgeous Japanese girl when she visited Britain as her part of the office swapping scheme that had taken Cassie to Tokyo. If Cassie hadn't been wanking him whilst they looked at increasingly naughty pictures of Megumi, he might have felt guilty about that thought.

Megumi had gone through a series of gun and swordplay poses, but now the weapons had gone. Her cape had been pulled forward, to hang straight down from her shoulders all the way to her knees. From her neck down to the belt of her hot pants was a strip of light brown skin. Her cleavage was barely exposed, but the knowledge that she had discarded her bikini top made the pose sexy.

In the next photo, the right side of the cape had been thrown back, exposing one of her small but perfect breasts, the dark brown nipple tilted up and slightly to one side. Cassie's fingers started moving faster on Noel's shaft. "I'm not the only one excited by these pictures." he managed to say.

Cassie stopped stroking for a moment and looked back and up with an embarrassed grin. "We have the same tastes, I guess."

"I'm not complaining." Noel said, as Cassie started slow strokes again.

Megumi had flung both wings of the cape back, to stand with hands on her hips displaying both breasts. She looked like she collapsed in giggles just after the photo was taken. Cassie was having problems keeping to a slow and steady rhythm. "She said she didn't want to send a video because it couldn't possibly be as good as the one we made." she said, talking as much to distract herself as anything else.

Obviously flushed from the laughter the previous picture had promised, Megumi now stood with the ends of her belt in either hand and the front of her hot pants open and spread far enough to show the top of a white thong. She must have changed the timer on her camera to take a photo every few seconds, because the next shot was the natural progression of her starting to push the tight shorts down. In the next, they were down to her knees, then she was leaning forwards as she pushed them down to her feet.

Noel had to take hold of Cassie's hand as she sped up again. It was an exquisite sensation, feeling her fingers sliding up and down his erection, but he didn't want to climax before he'd seen all the pictures.

"She actually apologised for 'only' sending us these pictures. That's so Japanese."

On screen, Megumi was pushing her thong down her legs, but she was leaning forward as she did it, so very little was on show. Cassie squeezed Noel's cock, but didn't start stroking again.

Megumi had straightened up. She had formed backwards V signs with her fingers and brought them up so that the tips framed her eyes as she stood at attention. Still wearing the boots and cape, she was fully exposed. Her waist curved in gently, then flared out at her hips, the line from her shoulders down and along her legs a sensuous curve.

She pouted for the camera, even though she must have known that the viewers' gaze would travel down, over her lovely little breasts and a lightly rounded stomach to the dark patch of her pubic hair and the lips under it.

Cassie's hand started moving on Noel's shaft again. He didn't stop her. "I told her about the video chats we had while I was in Japan. I think I've convinced her to do one with us next week." Cassie said, pausing to squeeze the bulbous purple head of Noel's cock. That news was going to make it hard for him to hold back the flood building at the base of his penis.

Megumi had sat on the futon and brought her feet up to perch the heels on its front edge. Her legs were raised and spread by her position, angling the neat slit of her opening toward the camera and parting the lips slightly. She was licking two fingers of her left hand, readying them for an obvious task.

In the next picture, the two fingers were between a different pair of lips, pushing into Megumi's pussy and opening it. She was staring straight at the camera, but there was a distance in her expression, the impression that her gaze was out of focus. Cassie's hand was moving faster again. Noel shifted his position, squirming under her fingers and trying to hold back the approaching orgasm.

Reading the signs, Cassie turned around, kneeling before Noel. She took him into her mouth and bobbed her head up and down, rubbing the flat of her tongue against the sensitive head of his erection. He didn't know whether to watch what she was doing or look at the screen. He glanced up, and his attention shifted completely to Megumi.

Two fingers still in herself, she was reaching to one side with her other hand. Noel just caught this picture before it quickly changed and revealed what she had been going for. The dildo was made from some soft material, so that it curved down from where she grasped its base. In the next picture, she had the realistically moulded head in her mouth, giving it a blow job.

When Cassie had been in Japan and she and Noel had made dirty video calls, he had eagerly watched her fellate a similar dildo, just like Megumi was doing on screen. Now, he was watching it re-enacted, remembering how hot it had been to watch first time, and had Cassie pleasuring him with her mouth. It was all too much.

Clasping the cushions of the couch, keeping himself from pushing up hard into Cassie's mouth, Noel came. Cassie gulped the semen down as it pumped out, pausing to swirl her tongue around the sensitive head and lick up any drips that might try to escape.

When Noel's cock had stopped twitching and there was no more juice to be licked off it, Cassie reverently lowered it to rest on the material of Noel's boxers. Turning, she looked at the television. "Oh my. I've got one of those. She recommended it, and I can see why."

On the screen, Megumi had hold of the dildo with both hands and was working it in her pussy. Her expression was pure bliss as successive photos showed it going in and out of her. Cassie reached over to her laptop and paused the playback. Turning back to Noel, she took his head between her hands and turned his view away from the erotic image on the television. She kissed him tenderly, then passionately.

When their lips parted, Cassie stared at Noel. Her cheeks had reddened, not all from the passion. "Is it okay? That I'm turned on by looking at another woman doing that. It doesn't freak you out?"

Now it was Noel's turn to guide Cassie into a kiss, a reassuring peck. "Did it feel like I was freaked out?"

Cassie smiled and blushed. Her hands ran up and down Noel's thighs and squeezed the muscle. "But what if.... What if I told you that it's got me thinking about making love with her?"

"With Megumi?" Noel glanced up at the screen. Cassie followed his gaze, and the conversation was derailed for a long moment as they both took in the image of a beautiful woman on the other side of the world freeze-framed in the throes of passion. Cassie nodded.

"It's just a fantasy. I mean.... I'm sure it's just a fantasy. I don't think she'd want to.... And I'm not saying her instead of you, or girls instead of men. I love you too much.... And I need your cock in my life."

Noel stopped Cassie with another kiss. "I love you, and I am so very glad that my cock is in your life." Cassie giggled. "And so what if you fancy a girl. I've fancied some guys in my time." Cassie went wide eyed, that was a revelation he hadn't shared before. "Judging by these pictures, the fantasy might just go both ways. We'll have to see what happens when she comes here. Just so long as I don't have to fight her for you. She may be small, but she's got swords."

"If anything does happen when she's here, you'll want to watch, won't you?"

"Hell, I'll want to join in."

"Dirty, dirty boy. Oh, look, you're still hard. Take those boxers off and I'll restart the slide show. I want to sit on you while we watch the rest of it."

* * *

NOEL HAD SET UP HIS computer and television so they could do the video call on them. The television would show the incoming image, whilst the computer's monitor displayed what was being transmitted. He'd hooked up the web cam on a long lead that Cassie had bought in Japan, because they could rove around the room with it and get close ups more easily. He had been thinking about what they were about to do, Cassie noted, the front of his loose climbing trousers were pushed out almost comically.

She was wearing his towelling bathrobe, fresh from the shower, with her hair still damp but brushed into some semblance of order. She drifted over to Noel and kissed him. "Nervous?" he asked, pretty much able to tell the answer from her body language as he laid hands gently on her hips.

"A little. And excited, obviously. I mean, we made the sex tape, and she's already seen that. But, we've never done it when we've known that someone was watching us."

"You've been pretty excited all the times when you've thought that people might be watching us."

"I know, I know. I'm just being silly."

"Should we call her, then?"

Cassie straightened the front of her robe, then worked out where the web cam was- clipped to the top of the television- and stood before it. "Let's call her."

Noel clicked the button to connect to Megumi's account, then stood beside Cassie. Checking the image on the computer screen, he put his hand about her waist and guided her two steps back so that they were better framed. As if spotting the bulge in the front of his trousers for the first time, he tried to pull the hem of his T-shirt down to cover it.

The ring icon on the television screen cycled for far too long, then connection was made. Coming from the late afternoon on the other side of the world, Megumi's face filled the screen. She blinked a few times, her big brown eyes wide, and smiled. "Konnichiwa Cassandra-san!"

"Ohayou, Megumi-san." Cassie gave a little bow to the screen.

"Of course, it is morning in England. Ohayou Noel-san, if I may be so informal."

Noel bowed to the screen. "Ohayou, um, Megumi-san. Please be informal. We are all friends here."

"And lovers." Cassie added.

"And lovers. It is a pleasure to meet you at last. Cassie has said so much about you, and, of course, there were the photos you sent."

Megumi blushed, and covered her face with her hands as she giggled. "You liked them?" she asked.

"I loved them. Your costumes were great as well."

"Thank you. I have spent all day wondering what costume I could wear to talk to you. It wasn't an easy decision. In the end, I chose this one." The reason that Megumi had been so close to the camera, so that only her face could be seen, became obvious. As she stepped backwards and stood up straight, the picture went blocky and confused as the software and connection tried to keep up with the rapidly changing picture. When it returned to normal, it was revealed that she was naked.

"Oh you beautiful girl." Cassie said. "Your costume is perfect. I think I should have the same one." She unfastened her robe and let it drop to the floor. Megumi stared at Cassie, it was possible to tell which side of the screen she was looking at. Noel glanced to the side, admiring his girlfriend's body. He couldn't blame Megumi for checking her out.

"You have shaved." Megumi said, pointing.

Cassie stroked the bare skin of her mound. "I did. Do you like it?"

"I do. It is very naughty. I could never do that." It was an oddly coy claim, considering the pictures Megumi had shared with them, and the very strange, cross-continents, tryst they were engaging in. Before Cassie had gone to Japan, this would have been an inconceivably bizarre fantasy scenario.

Noel had turned his attention to their long distance lover in Japan. He only had Cassie's description to go on for Megumi's height- just tall enough to reach her nose, which meant she would come up to just above his chin. She was perfectly proportioned, slim, with a nicely turned in waist, shapely arms and legs and small breasts. Almost, Noel glanced to his side again, like a scaled down version of his girlfriend. He was so turned on, looking back and forth at these beauties, that he was almost dizzy.

Cassie was looking back at Noel, smiling. She nodded toward the screen, and he realised Megumi was looking at him as well. "Someone still has their clothes on." Cassie said.

"I suppose I should take them off, then." Noel quickly pulled the T-shirt over his head and tossed it away. As he hooked his thumb into the waistband of his trousers, he saw Megumi step back and sit on the futon. He bent over as he pushed them down and stepped out of them. When he straightened up again, Megumi tilted her head, studied what she saw on her screen, then smiled broadly. Higher pitched than before, she said something in Japanese.

Cassie burst out laughing. Completely lost, Noel turned to her. She had a hand over her mouth to hide her own silly grin, but she said, "It's okay, it was very complimentary. I'm not sure I can properly translate it, though."

"I may have compared you to a horse. I was using slang, and I think Cassandra-san is correct that it would be hard to translate the phrase exactly. You have a marvellous penis Noel-san." Megumi said, still grinning widely.

"Thank you very much. You have a marvellous.... everything. You are truly gorgeous."

For a while they all just looked at each other, enjoying their shared nudity over the internet. Cassie turned to face Noel, but still glanced at the television screen. She asked a question in Japanese, and Megumi leant forward to pay more attention. "I would like to see that." she said.

"See what?" Noel asked. That the two women could communicate in a language he didn't understand was disconcerting. A bit like being blindfolded, he thought, he couldn't be sure what was coming next.

Cassie took his hand and turned him to face her. Then she gracefully dropped to her knees, in what could have been the most erotic curtsy ever. She took his shaft in one hand and cradled his balls in the other, then stared up at him. "Cassandra-san asked if I would like to see her give you oral sex." Megumi said. She reached down for something just below her web cam's view. "I will try to do to this what she is doing to you." she said, holding up the dildo she had used in the photo set.

"Okay." Noel said, not up to forming a longer answer. He watched Megumi, who watched Cassie and tried to match her actions. Turning slightly to the side, Megumi held up the dildo, one hand around the base and another around the shaft, and moved it toward her mouth.

Noel felt the warmth of a tongue licking up his shaft, from base to tip. A moment later, Megumi's tongue did the same to the dildo. It was like he was getting a virtual blow job from Japan. He glanced at the computer monitor and got a view of what was happening in the room, just as Cassie took as much as she could manage into his mouth. This was why people put mirrors up in their bedrooms, he thought.

Megumi had the dildo down her throat almost to the base, her head tilted back. Noel looked down just as Cassie glanced at the television. Her eyes went wide at the sight of her friend deep throating a fake erection. That was a skill she didn't have, and Noel fancied he could see a hint of envy in her expression.

Knowing she wasn't going to take Noel any deeper, Cassie drew her lips back to the head with a slurp. Across continents, they heard an echo as Megumi copied her actions. After kissing and sucking around the head for a while, Cassie turned to the web cam. "You must teach me how to do that."

"To take the whole length? It will be a pleasure." Megumi waggled the dildo, dripping with her saliva, and asked, "What shall we do next with our men?"

"Would you like him in you?" Cassie said.

"Oh yes, yes I would." Megumi studied the room on her screen. "If he sits on your bench seat, you can sit on him. Would you face me, so I can see him going in and out of you?"

"Of course."

"I think I should move the camera." Noel said. He stepped up to the television, and Megumi giggled as she got a close up of his hard on. When he unclipped the camera from the screen, he gave her an even better view, running it up and down as close as he could get without the shot going out of focus. Megumi whispered out a few complimentary words in Japanese and Cassie laughed along.

There was a tripod at the ready, and the web cam fitted in place on top of it. Noel stood the tripod where he had been moments before, and checked the view on the computer monitor, then moved it back toward the television a little. Satisfied with the framing, he walked over to the couch and dropped onto it. "I'm ready for my close up." he said.

Cassie stood before him, and, before she could turn to face the camera, her reached up. Sliding his fingers over the soft skin of her thighs, he found his way to the warm lips of her sex. They parted easily to the two fingers that slid into her, as her legs parted and she crouched a little to force herself down onto them. She was as excited by this as he was, unsurprisingly.

Turning Cassie around, Noel supported her as she lowered herself onto him. Reaching down, she found him and, fingers just below the purple glans, guided his shaft into her. There was a moment's pause, as she changed the angle of her hips ever so slightly so that he filled her easily, then she slid down his length. Buried deep in her, Noel reached around and played his fingers, still slick with her juices, around her mons and then teasingly over the hood hiding her clitoris. She sighed and wriggled at the strokes.

They paused to take a look at the screen. Megumi was watching them intently, fascinated and gently stroking the dildo, giving a hand job to her rubber lover. Realising she was being watched, she sat back. "Let me feed him into me." she said.

Noel's fingers circled around Cassie's clit and his free hand came up to squeeze a breast and tweak the nipple. Her hips started rotating, pressing his cock against the tight walls of her vagina. All the while, they watched as Megumi stretched out and ran the head of the dildo up and down her slit. The lips parted and moved over the rubber glans before it lodged and found its way deeper into her.

Megumi looked at Noel and Cassie, making eye contact, somehow, across the internet. She dared them to look at her face and not what she was doing, knowing they could never resist. The dildo drew slowly out of her as she grinned at the way Noel's and Cassie's glances moved back and forth between face and pussy.

Cassie raised herself from Noel's lap, trying to match the speed and depth of the dildo's movements in Megumi. She dropped back down quickly as the other woman thrust it back into herself, then began the slow lifting again. Noel moved his hands to rest on her waist, ready to hold her up if she needed it.

As Megumi and Cassie sped up, it was obvious their climaxes were drawing closer at speed. They slipped out of rhythm, Cassie having to slow down as she started to get tremors and shivers up and down her legs whilst Megumi moved the dildo faster and faster. Her cries sounded distant as her head tilted back, but then she came, and seemed to fold herself around the dildo, and her cry shot up in volume and pitch.

Cassie watched, fascinated, as her friend dropped forwards off the futon onto her knees. Megumi's gorgeous face, flushed and with just a hint of perspiration from the effort, filled the screen again. Her mouth was open and her eyes closed as she panted out her excitement.

Noel's fingers worked around and down to Cassie's mons again, then down, to circle her clitoris with growing speed and pressure. His other arm held her around the chest as she squirmed. Megumi's eyes opened slowly as she heard Cassie's approaching orgasm. She smiled at the sight of her friend in ecstasy. Cassie's eyes were barely open, but she could see the pleasure Megumi was taking in watching her, and it pushed her over the edge. Grasping the arm Noel had around her chest, she rotated her hips and squeezed him as the shudders ran through her body.

Cassie laid back against Noel as the shudders of aftershocks moved through her. He ran his hands over her body, squeezing her breasts and stroking her thighs and sides, but avoiding her still sensitive clitoris. She made a happy sound, practically a purr, at the after play.

"You are both so beautiful." Megumi said, her voice low, as if worried she would disturb them.

"Thank you." Cassie said, just as quietly, with the huskiness of a recent climax.

"Can I ask, Noel-san, have you ejaculated yet?"

It wasn't such an odd question, in the circumstances. "Not yet." Noel managed to say, "But I'm close."

"Would you.... Could I ask if I could see it?"

"Oh, that'll be so hot." Cassie said, stirring. "I'll help." She lifted herself, carefully, off Noel, then knelt in front of the camera. Looking at the computer screen, she adjusted her location for the best picture and gestured for Noel to join her.

"Could you ejaculate on Cassandra-san's beautiful breasts?" Megumi asked. "That will be so exciting."

Cassie took hold of Noel's hard on, tugging it down a little to help aim it at her breasts. Holding it with one hand, she started moving the other up and down slowly, sliding a little on the juices it was coated with. He tried to hold still as she took him ever closer to climax.

Noel's thigh muscles felt like they were vibrating as he held himself up against the building orgasm. He looked at the screen. Megumi was watching them closely, but the way she bobbed back and forward, it was obvious that she was working the dildo inside herself again. She squeaked as another climax hit her, then bit her lower lip as she kept up the pumping actions, aiming to stay on the plateau of orgasm.

Cassie could tell from the way Noel's cock felt as if it was bulging out, that he was about to climax. She lifted herself, placing her cleavage closer to the head. With a grunt, Noel came. He thrust forward as he pumped semen out. Resisting the temptation to clamp her lips around the head and suck up the sticky liquid, Cassie watched the white blobs shooting, and then dribbling out of his cock onto her breasts. Far away, Megumi called out as she came again.

For a long time, they were all quiet, recovering and savouring the sensations. Noel ran his fingers through Cassie's hair and she rubbed her head against his hand like a cat. She looked up and smiled, then they turned to the television.

Megumi had a happy, dazed look. She was sat on the floor, back against the futon, smiling. "Next time we do this, we must be in the same room." she said after a while.

"We must? You want to do that?" Cassie asked.

"Oh yes, yes please. Well, it's nearly three months until I am in England. Maybe we will have to do it again this way before then, or I may explode."

"Let's start planning now."

So they did, talking about what they wanted to do for hours. They didn't even have time to get dressed, and, before long, Cassie and Noel were making love again as Megumi perched on the edge of her futon and watched. She wanted so much to be in the same room as them, and could hardly wait until she could visit and join in.

Don't miss out!

Visit the website below and you can sign up to receive emails whenever Mary Tales publishes a new book. There's no charge and no obligation.

https://books2read.com/r/B-A-XESE-HSQO

BOOKS 2 READ

Connecting independent readers to independent writers.

Did you love *Cassie Gets it On*? Then you should read *Love By The Book*[1] by Mary Tales!

*Contains several explicit scenes. Over 18s only.*Samantha is in her final year as an undergraduate. She wants to do well, get on a Masters degree and then do a PhD, so she doesn't have the time to start a new relationship. She's got a boyfriend in another city, though he's a bit useless, and a vibrator by the bed. She'll be fine.But then she meets Greg. He's nearly twice her age, but she can't deny she's attracted to him. Then she starts reading his books, and they fuel her fantasies and have her wondering if she should make the time for a change of lover.After years of struggling, Greg has struck it lucky with his writing. He's earning more than he could have hoped, so it's a terrible time for writer's block to strike. His muse has started the Christmas break early, it would seem. But at least there is beer, mulled wine, and a gorgeous younger woman to take his mind off all that.Told by both Samantha and Greg, Love By The Book is sweet, funny and very, very hot.

---

1. https://books2read.com/u/mgrLYq

2. https://books2read.com/u/mgrLYq

Also by Mary Tales

Jiggles
Jiggles and the Test Pilot
Jiggles and the Archaeologists
Jiggles and the Flying Boats
Jiggles and the Black Shaft

Love By The Book
Love By The Book
Love The Weekend

Mary Tales Collections
Contact Adventures
Contact Adventures 2 - First Timers
Cassie Gets it On
The Adventures of Jiggles

Mary Tales Shorts Collections
Mary Tales Shorts Collection 1
Mary Tales Omnibus

Meet The Gang
Meet The Gang

Queen Leena
Queen Leena 1: The Queen's Men